Becoming Kira

Sometimes life gives you choices

A novella by

gloria C. Bishop

Copyright © 2015 by Gloria C Bishop
All rights reserved.
ISBN: 978-0-9940805-0-9
Cover Model: Carla Coles
Photographer: Scott Coles
Model Accessories: Inside My Wicked Wardrobe
Design assistance: Christy Bernard
Editing: Barbara Storey

Gloria C. Bishop

DEDICATION

To my daughter who is a wonderful, creative and beautiful teenager whose support and love I am intensely lucky to have. She teaches me every day about following my dreams and inspires me to be a better person. Her openhearted approach to life and the way she cares about everyone reminds me to love those around me and accept them as they are. Love you baby girl.

And

To my son, whose sense of humour and unerring ability to pun anything, keeps me from getting too serious. The way he overcomes obstacles and has become the sensitive, amazing young man he has become, teaches me that we can all do anything we set our minds to. I love you. Although it is a good thing I also have a sense of humour or the comment, "Its only romance Mom, it doesn't really count" might have upset me.

ACKNOWLEDGEMENTS

I want to take a moment to thank all the wonderful supporters I have around me. I am incredibly lucky to have a group of artistic, creative and helpful friends who have not only helped by beta reading for me but also by listening to me constantly ramble on about the world that exists only in my head. Tracy, Marilyn, Leah, and Laureen, you guys are the best.

To my writers group, The Imagined Book Club, Carla, Adam, and Barb thank you for all your mental support and also for reading, helping edit and advising me.

Thank you also to my wonderful husband Bill, for the unending support and inspiration and for allowing me to follow my dreams with unwavering support and confidence.

1 CHAPTER ONE

*M*atronly? *Who the hell did he think he was?* Kira wasn't even forty yet and that rat bastard of an ex-husband said she looked like she should be wearing muumuus, granny panties, and a utilitarian bra. He hadn't hesitated to yell out that she dressed more like his mother than a woman he would find attractive. Of course, that was right before he left her for a miniskirt-wearing, marathon-running twenty-two-year-old, whose ass was still perfect and her breasts perky without the support of a bra.

Kira shook her head, trying to dislodge the memories. It had been five months since Steve had left. Five months of being alone. Five months of tears and recriminations, none of which changed the facts: she was on her own. They had never had children, thinking their lives were better without them, and now Kira wasn't sure if that was a good thing or not. Sometimes she felt it was better that no one else was being hurt by the collapse of her marriage. Other times she longed for someone to share her misery with, a child who would be hers even if she was slightly overweight, who would love her even when she got old. But that was not to be her fate.

She was a thirty-eight-year-old newly divorced woman. The last few months had been instructional at least. Being forced to look at herself honestly and decide whether Steve was telling the truth, or only spewing filth to avoid his own feelings of guilt, had been revealing.

Kira knew she wasn't perfect—no one would call her curvy hour glass body perfect. Her breasts were large and unruly (they didn't like following simple instructions, like stay *inside* the bra), her frame wasn't petite. At five foot eight she stood heads above all those perfectly perky little pixies, looking more like an Amazon than a sexy woman. Her once rich auburn hair had faded to a softer brown and her face had laugh lines. She was, after all, thirty eight.

So although she knew she could stand to lose a few pounds, and that she was in no way, shape, or form a twenty-year-old any longer, she also knew she wasn't too bad.

The only thing Steve had been right about was her sense of fashion. Over the last couple of years she had allowed comfort to become more important than style. Her sagging, too big yoga pants should never have seen the outside of her apartment, yet had become the uniform she wore most days. Her flip flops and running shoes, the go-to shoes: Kira couldn't remember the last time she wore anything that resembled a heel, when once upon a time that was all she wore. Mind you, that had been Steve's preference; he couldn't stand it when she wore high heels and towered over his five-foot-ten-inch tall frame, so to make him happy she had stopped wearing footwear that made her any taller.

Her hair had grown straggly and was worn most days in a ponytail down her back, because it was easier. Her legs got shaved sporadically at best. Although she was always fastidious about snatch styling her hoo-hah (because nothing in the world was worth growing a 1970s bush), she occasionally let her legs slide. Her makeup drawer was nearly empty except for some simple mascara and clear lip gloss.

Today was the day she changed that. Kira stood in front of Clips, the most exclusive salon here in Chatelane. Glancing at her watch, she took a breath and stepped inside. Immediately the air conditioning hit her, cooling her overheated skin as the soothing music and soft lighting relaxed her.

Kira stepped up to the desk, a monstrosity of glass and metal. A young man looked up and smiled. His black hair had way too much product in it, as it stood precariously on end, defying all laws of nature and fashion. But his eyes were kind and his smile one thousand watts, showing the benefits of modern dentistry.

"Hi, I'm Kira, I have a three o'clock."

"Of course, darling." The receptionist had a drawl that sounded somewhat southern as he slurred the word 'dawlin' and fiddled with the computer for a few moments before turning back to her. "You're with Lindsay. She should be ready for you any minute. Can I get you a coffee? Or a water?"

"No thanks." Kira smiled and sank into one of the comfortable chairs, grabbing a magazine to flip through while she waited.

Bare moments had passed when Lindsay approached. She was in her late twenties, another of the pert little things, maybe topping five foot. Her porcelain skin was made up perfectly and a broad smile slashed the bright red mouth in half. Her hair (as expected of a hairstylist) was stunning. A rich curtain of white blonde with streaks of blue and purple seemingly placed at random.

"Kira ?" she asked, holding out her hand.

Kira stood, once again towering over another woman; regardless, she smiled, nodded, and shook the woman's hand.

"I'm Lindsay. Let's head to the back." She led Kira through the reception area and into the bowels of the salon. She indicated a chair with a graceful hand and Kira sat down, stealthily avoiding looking at herself in the plethora of mirrors.

"What is it we are doing for you today, Kira?" Lindsay asked.

"Um. A haircut?" Kira answered.

Lindsay laughed pleasantly, a sound Kira imagined fairies made while passing wind, before speaking sternly, as though to a child. "No, sweetie, one doesn't come to Clips for a 'haircut'." She sneered the word as though it tasted bad in her mouth. "You come to Clips for a hair style."

"Okay then, a style. A trim. Maybe a couple inches off." Kira met Lindsay's blue eyes with dismay.

"When you booked the appointment, I am sure you said you wanted a change. Is that not correct?" Kira nodded miserably; she never felt comfortable being decisive. She and Steve used to take hours just trying to decide where to go to eat, since neither of them could choose.

"Well then, sweetie, how about you let me take charge? I am the best. I can make you look like a million bucks, if you'll let me have free reign. Let's make you feel like the beautiful woman you deserve to feel like." Instead of being condescending, her words reassured Kira.

Lindsay was smiling softly at Kira, whose eyes were suspiciously damp as she nodded and whispered. "Your choice then. Just make me different. Give me the full treatment."

With that, Lindsay grinned and took over.

2 CHAPTER TWO

A few hours later Kira exited the salon; the previously warm day had now cranked up the humidity, so it felt like walking into a hazy corner in hell. It was so hot it was hard to catch a breath, but she reached a hand up to her hair with a smile. Nothing could make her unhappy at this moment. No longer a boring brown, her hair was a rich shade of red with black and blond streaks added for interest. The colour alone was different than anything she ever would have thought to put on herself and the style was an asymmetrical bob, buzzed in the back and longer in the front. A heavy fall of bangs drew attention to her eyes; the subtle smoky shadows made the green tones in them appear emerald. She had been waxed, plucked, dyed, styled and had her makeup done.

A spring in her step, Kira turned towards her car and a glint of light caught her eye. It was coming from the sign for ZigZag, a women's clothing store, which she had always considered too young for her.

Glaring at the memory of her closed mindedness, Kira changed direction and stalked straight into the store.

Unlike the salon, ZigZag had rock music playing loud enough to be slightly uncomfortable. There were racks upon racks of brightly coloured clothes. Jeans, dresses, shoes, T-shirts, tank tops, sequins. A woman's heaven.

Kira thought about turning around and running; after all she had no idea where to start. Straightening her back with determination, Kira moved further into the store.

An eager young employee came up to help her. Within minutes she was ensconced in a change room, trying on item after item.

She tugged on a pair of dark blue skinny jeans. Her opinion of skinny jeans was that they only belonged on teenyboppers and wouldn't look right on her super tall frame. She was wrong. Prancing in front of the mirror, she twisted and turned, checking out her ass. It looked fabulous, tight and high, while her legs looked like they reached her armpits. Kira thought these were exactly what she needed.

"How are those?" The employee's voice came from the other side of the door.

"I love them!" Kira exclaimed, happily running her fingers over the tops of her thighs. "But I need a top to go with them."

"I know just the thing. I'll be right back."

A moment later a shiny black top was flung over the top of the door. Gingerly, Kira shook it out. A sleeveless blouse with a light sprinkling of sparkles and strategically placed seams met her gaze.

"Before you try that on, you need a good black bra to go with it." The young girl's voice came again.

"Oh. Do you have bras here?" Kira asked.

"We sure do. What size?" Kira could hear the smile in her voice.

"36 double d."

"Coming up."

While Kira waited, she slid on the pair of shoes she had instinctively grabbed. These were unlike anything she had ever owned before. Black, green, and purple material in a delightful sugar skull pattern covered the platform heels that would make her four inches taller. She stood gazing into the mirror at the six-foot-tall woman looking back at her. The heels were a perfect fit.

"Here you go!" The cheerful voice caught her attention as a bra was thrust over the door. Kira took it, thanking the employee as she struggled to put the lacy contraction on. With raw determination she forced her uncooperative breasts into submission inside the formed cups. She then slid the slinky material of the shirt over her head and sighed.

It was silky and soft, caressing her skin in a way she had been longing for. The scoop neckline and new bra emphasized a bosom that was anything but matronly.

Kira grinned and stepped out of the dressing room, to look in the larger mirrors in the main portion of the store.

"Whoa!" The employee exclaimed, in a throwback that brought *Bill and Ted's Excellent Adventure* to Kira's mind. "That looks great on you."

Kira stared at herself in awe; it was like the past few hours had erased ten years off her life. She looked young, carefree, and hot.

"I'll take it." Kira whispered. "Is it possible for me to wear it now?"

The employee nodded and led her to the till.

She paid the bill with a twinge at the grand total, but determined not to let her innate thriftiness hold her back now. She was scheduled to start her new job at The Chatelane *Herald* in a couple of weeks; yet another step to her independence. Until then her alimony paid for everything she needed, and her frugal nature had ensured she always had extra. After stuffing her yoga pants, flip flops and T-shirt into the store bag, Kira left wearing the new outfit.

Walking down the block, she noticed a few looks being tossed her way and she smiled happily. When she reached her car, she unlocked the door and tossed her bag in the back.

With a sigh she threw herself into the driver's seat. She didn't want to go home yet. Had she spent all day getting done over to look like a brand new woman, clothes and everything, just to go sit at home alone and watch *Doctor Who*?

Just as Kira was debating where to go her stomach growled, making her decision easy. She dropped the car into drive and sped expertly across town to her favourite restaurant, Dominic's.

At first when Steve had left her, she found it virtually impossible to go out and eat alone. The horror at having to answer, "Yes a table for one," overwhelmed her. She couldn't stand the thought of going out to any of the places they had gone to as a couple, but after nearly a month of only fast food and her limited culinary skills, she had finally caved. In a fluke of craving real food that she hadn't prepared herself, Kira had finally ventured out.

Dominic's was a warm and inviting Italian restaurant, set on the outskirts of Chatelane. It was all decked out in red and butter yellow, with comfy seats and food that was to die for. There were private tables ringing the restaurant area, where you could sit in groups of up to six. Booths in the bar area offered more privacy. The thing that Kira liked most, and what drew her back again and again, was in the main dining room. There was always at least one "family" table. It sat up to ten guests and anyone could sit there. She had met couples who wanted some conversation, singles who didn't want to feel alone, and older folks who liked to meet new people.

The family table had been started by the owner, and her first time there she had sat with him for hours talking and drinking wine. Dominic—although he preferred to be called Dom—had explained to her that he missed the big Italian family meals he had grown up with, where everyone was talking and laughing around a big communal table. So when he opened his restaurant, he wanted to give his diners a choice.

So far the family table was a hit; every time Kira went it was always occupied. In the past her intentions had always been to not eat, or be alone, but today as she pulled into the parking lot she finally felt lighter, actually wanting to meet new people.

She strolled into the building and waited at the hostess station. She could see the family table and was slightly disappointed to only see one patron there.

The hostess approached with a smile on her face. "Good afternoon."

"Hi," Kira returned the grin. "I'll just sit at the family

table today, please."

The young girl nodded and happily led her towards the big table. Dom popped out of the kitchen and, spying her, intercepted the two of them before they made it across the restaurant.

"Kira. Your hair!" She turned and looked at his tall frame as he approached. Dom was an attractive man in his mid-forties. His hair was still coal black and he wore it slightly longer than was in fashion currently. He had piercing blue eyes ringed with a set of lashes any woman would have killed to have.

"Dom." Kira smiled sincerely; Dom had become her closest ally while her marriage fell apart. She had talked his ear off and used his shoulder to cry on, on more than one occasion, usually when she was three sheets to the wind, but he had been supportive nonetheless. She had recently found herself looking at him as a man rather than just a friend, and that was when Kira knew she had to move on. Although he never talked about his wife, his left hand attested to the fact that he was married. And Kira would never dream of stepping out with a married man. Dom was just a friend.

"So, what do you think?" she asked and waved an arm at her new outfit and hair.

Dom paused and looked at her. "You look different," he said quietly, his Italian accent whispering across her skin, as he kissed both her cheeks. "And as always, beautiful."

Kira rolled her eyes. "Different? That doesn't sound good."

"Yes, different. The hair colour is… unexpected. You didn't need to change the way you looked."

"I wanted to be different." Kira clarified.

"There was no need for you to change." Dom frowned at her.

"You were the one who told me, just the other night, to be daring and try something new." Kira was exasperated.

The last time Kira had been here, she and Dom had drunk wine late into the night, talking. He had told her to be bold.

To make choices she never would have done before. And so she had.

Dom was staring at her as though she had three horns for daring to want a fresh look. He wasn't going to ruin her high with his attitude. She liked the way she looked and he could kiss her ass if he didn't.

"Yes. But I didn't mean…." Dom trailed off.

"Well. I like it." Kira snapped. "Now if you don't mind, I'm starving."

With her head held high, she deliberately did not stomp, as that would be childish; instead she walked loudly to the family table, and slowly sank down onto one of the seats across from the table's one inhabitant. He was young; Kira placed him at around twenty-two, his blond hair buzzed in a military-style cut. He had wide dark-brown eyes and a cheerful smile.

"I'm Kira." She held out a hand.

"Hi, I'm Michael." He shook her hand over the table; his eyes took a slow stroll over her hair and down to her chest, then back to her face, his eyes showing a pure masculine appreciation. "I'm glad you came, I was beginning to wonder if I'd have to eat alone."

"Well, you don't have to wonder anymore." The waitress approached and Kira turned to her.

"I'll have a glass of your house red, and whatever the daily special is." Then she turned back to Michael.

"Have you been here before?" She couldn't help the twinge of lust she felt as Michael leaned back and stretched. His black button-down shirt pulled tight over beautifully sculpted biceps. High cheekbones and full lips gave him a hypnotic appearance. Overall, he looked as though he had been chiselled out of granite and then brought to life. She shook her head internally; it had been too long since she'd felt like a woman, if she was finding men as young as Michael attractive. She didn't think she was quite ready to be classified as a cougar and going after a twenty-two-year-old would definitely put her in that class.

"Actually I am kinda a regular here." Michael smiled. "But I know this must be your first time here. I would never forget a woman like you." Michael dropped his head to his hand, muttering. "Oh my god. That came out sounding so corny. I am totally ashamed."

Kira laughed. "It did sound pretty corny, but I know you didn't mean it that way so I'll forgive you."

"How do you know I didn't mean it that way?" Michael straightened, his eyes twinkling with merriment.

"Because I am old enough to be your mother." Kira scoffed, pursing her lips, refusing to acknowledge her screeching, horny loins.

"Not a chance. You're what, thirty?"

"Oh, thank you so much for thinking that." Kira smiled. "I am somewhat older than thirty. And you're lucky if you hit twenty-two."

"First things first. There is nothing more attractive than an older woman." His eyes brightened as they looked at Kira, a flush spreading over her cheeks. "And second, I thank you for thinking that." Michael's one eyebrow arched, causing Kira's libido to stand up and sing. "But I must disappoint you; I just turned twenty-six. It's the buzz cut, it makes me look younger." He ran a hand over his lightly stubbled hair.

Twelve years younger wasn't as bad as she had originally thought. Instead of cougar material, it put her in lynx status; that wasn't *quite* as offensive. "Okay. So you're not a baby." Kira amended, looking at him through her lashes as the waitress arrived with her glass of wine.

Kira had never flirted so blatantly with anyone before. It was like the new look had given her a courage she hadn't previously possessed. Now that she was single she had better learn how to talk to strangers and how to flirt; tonight was as good a night as any to start testing the waters.

She was a free woman, able to do whatever, whenever she wanted. Hell, if she decided to hump the entire eastern seaboard there was no one to stop her. Her thighs and other unmentionable body parts would probably hurt, but she was free.   For the first time since Steve, she felt a touch of anticipation.

She took a slow, appreciative sip of her wine, closing her eyes and enjoying the tartness bursting on her tongue. When she opened her eyes, her gaze locked with Michael's. "So Michael, what do you do for a living?"

3 CHAPTER THREE

An hour and a half later, Kira still sat at the family table. She had just finished her dessert, a decadent chocolate tiramisu. Several other diners had joined the table and the conversation was loud and boisterous.

Kira had gotten appreciative looks several times throughout the course of the meal and had been complimented lavishly by men and women both. She felt like a million bucks, just as the hairstylist had promised. Her new flirty attitude seemed to be well received, although she was very careful not to spend too much time talking to anyone who appeared to be taken.

Kira's gaze kept being drawn back to the young and oh so pretty Michael. Every time she looked at him she found him staring back at her. Her cheeks flushed; it had been so long since she'd felt appreciated as a woman. Hell, she had burnt out the motor of yet another B.O.B last week, and her wallet regretted not buying stocks in Duracell when she had had the chance. Her lustful urges was sorely underused at the moment.

She noticed as she handed the waitress her credit card that Michael had motioned for his bill as well. "It was very nice meeting you, Michael," she said.

"You too, Kira. I haven't had that much fun eating dinner here, well, ever." His plump lips curved upwards in a gentle smile.

Kira signed the credit card slip with a flourish, thrilled with the evening. Just as she was about to say her good-byes, the previously empty chair beside her slid out. She turned to see Dom sitting down.

"Kira." His voice was a low grumble. "I'm sorry I haven't been able to come over before now. I had problems in the kitchen tonight." He took a breath and continued in a quiet voice. "I wanted to apologize."

"It's okay." Kira said, even though she was still upset that he didn't seem to appreciate her initiative and the changes she had made to be happier.

"It's really not. You shocked me. And you do look stunning. No matter how you style or colour your hair, you will always be beautiful. So I am sorry, and I hope you can forgive me." Dom's blue eyes drilled into Kira's and she stood, ignoring the impossible but irresistible pull from the taken man.

"I forgive you, Dom. I shouldn't expect married men to compliment me anyways." She shrugged lightly and turned away, barely registering the confused look on Dom's face as she left with a casual wave to the table.

Once outside she took a deep breath, catching the humidity of the summer air in her mouth like cotton candy. Although she had enjoyed herself, she was grateful to be heading home, where the air conditioning would cool her body and still her lust. The door banged shut behind her and she turned to see Michael strolling out of the restaurant. His body was a thing of beauty to behold: pure, unadulterated manliness, with bulk and muscles in all the right places.

"Hey." He smiled, his teeth looking even whiter in the soft darkness of the evening. "Um, Kira, we seemed to get along so great—I was wondering if maybe you wanted to go get a drink? I would suggest a movie, but we"—he glanced at her watch—"are a bit too late."

"How about Coffee Climate? It's open late and just a few blocks away." Kira had spent many lonely nights in that coffee shop. It was just down the street from her place and had the best cappuccinos in town.

"I know the place." Michael grinned, happiness exuding

from his eyes. "Meet you there in five?"

Kira nodded and got into her car, quickly starting the engine and flicking the a/c on full, while she unwound the windows, hoping for a little relief. She looked up in time to have her jaw drop at the hotness that was Michael as he flung a leg over a massive motorbike. His thighs hugged the machine as it roared to life beneath him. It felt like Kira's inner harlot had been started at the same time as the motorcycle. He waved and pulled on his helmet before shifting into gear and roared out of the parking lot with Kira following, trying to wrench her eyes away from the hotness of Michael's ass.

What am I thinking? Kira winced. It was crazy; she was going out for coffee with a baby, a bare toddler, whom she had just met. No matter how nice he seemed, he could be a mass murderer. Kira laughed out loud; the idea of a serial killer in Chatelane was pretty far-fetched, let alone one who preyed on middle-aged, divorced women. Add to that the fact that she had just had dinner with him in a very public atmosphere, which pretty much crossed criminal off the list of who he might be.

It's just coffee, I can always let him down easy if I want to. I am single and no one will get hurt. So what if I think he's a total hunk stick? I can do what I want.

With those thoughts firmly in mind, Kira smiled, looking forward to more conversation with the intriguing Michael.

4 CHAPTER FOUR

Michael and Kira stood outside, relieved to finally have some respite from the heat. It was two o'clock in the morning, and a cool breeze had blown the humidity from the day away. They had been asked, ever so politely, to leave Coffee Climate after spending nearly five hours there, talking and laughing. The staff wanted to go home.

Kira was impressed by Michael; he was an incredibly charming man, whose smile always caused a flutter in her nether regions. For a twenty-six-year-old he had an incredible head on his shoulders, having completed his apprenticeship several years ago and now working as a carpenter. But his passion was his art; Michael had shown her several pictures of his artwork and Kira was blown away. He sculpted beautiful pieces from wood.

"I'm so glad I can finally breathe!" Kira moaned, taking a deep breath and closing her eyes.

"For sure. That heat was unbearable." Michael also blissfully breathed deep, sighing in happiness.

Kira leaned against the building, the brick cool against the bare skin on her arms. She tilted her head and closed her eyes, revelling in the slight breeze that brushed against her skin. The dark, cool night relaxed her mind and her body. A half smile tilted her mouth, and she turned to thank Michael; opening her eyes, the words died on her lips.

He stood, inches away from her, intensity written on every part of his body. His brown eyes reflecting the light from the street lamps as his hand reached up and caressed the side of her neck. His palm paralleled her jaw bone with a gentleness Kira wouldn't have thought possible.

Her lips parted as her eyes flew to his, unable to believe this young man was looking at her with such lust.

"I've wanted to do this all night." His voice was a rumble, low in his chest, as he leaned in and kissed her.

His plump lips gently touched hers, softly but insistently plucking at her lower lip until she parted her mouth, granting him access. His tongue swept over hers as his other hand gripped the side of her face, tilting her for better access. His thumb swept across her neck, tracing her pulse point as he laid siege to her mouth. She could faintly taste the cappuccino he had finished earlier, along with a taste that was pure Michael, spicy and strong.

Kira felt electric shocks racing across her skin, a throbbing starting low in her body. It had been so long since she had felt the curve of lust, the blood-boiling excitement of a man touching her. She moaned and leaned in, deepening the kiss to new levels. Her hands automatically threaded themselves around his neck as he leaned into her, his hard body pressing into hers. The heat from his body contrasted with the coolness of the brick behind her.

For a few minutes they lost themselves in each other. They explored each other's mouths with hungry passion, filled with need. Finally they broke apart, breathing heavily, and Michael leaned his forehead against Kira's. Her heels made them the same height, their bodies fit together like puzzle pieces.

"Wow." Michael sighed.

"No kidding." Kira's laugh was shaky as she tried to catch her breath.

They pulled away slightly, and Kira led the way towards her home. Earlier Kira had explained how close she lived and Michael had insisted on getting her home safely when they left.

As they started out, Michael slid his hand into Kira's,

fingers entwining as though they belonged. They didn't speak, just walked in silence, the sexual tension enough to fill the air.

Finally they stepped up to the low-rise townhouse that Kira lived in. "This is me." She turned toward Michael. "Thank you for a great night."

Michael looked at her, intensity evident in every line of his body. "It doesn't have to end yet," he murmured, running his fingers lightly over her new hairstyle.

She stared up at him, eyes wide with shock. She had never slept with a man on the first night they met. Hell, she'd never slept with anyone except Steve, who had been her first and only lover.

The thought both excited and terrified her. However, she also knew it was time to move on. She had made great strides today and she really didn't want the night to end yet. Her body was thrumming with an energy she had forgotten existed within her. She wanted this younger man more than she would have thought possible. And he wanted her back. Even if it was purely a sexual thing and nothing more, she could accept that. It was time to dip her toes into the waters of singledom.

With trepidation, Kira nodded and, taking Michael's hand, led him into her apartment. She desperately hoped sex was like riding a bike: that a person never forgot how.

Once inside Kira walked into the small living room, straightening the end table, grabbing the old T-shirt off the floor and throwing it into a corner.

"Do you want a drink?" she asked, her nerves overwhelming her as she tried to stop herself from shaking.

"Relax," Michael soothed her. He stood behind Kira, rubbing her arms and shoulders until she felt the nervousness lessen; she leaned back against the width of Michael's chest.

"I've never done anything like this before," Kira whispered, afraid that Michael would laugh at her inexperience.

"Don't worry about it, we'll take it as it comes. There's no right or wrong here." His voice brushed lightly at her hair.

She closed her eyes, losing herself in the soft whisper of his words and the gentle caresses up and down her arms. His lips brushed the shell of her ear as he spoke. "You undo me. So beautiful."

His hands travelled from her arms to her waist, holding her and creating slow spirals with his fingertips through her lightweight shirt. Gooseflesh travelled across her skin as her head fell back to rest on Michael's shoulder. His lips travelled in a light path along her neck, lightly kissing and suckling until Kira felt like she was on fire. Finally his hands cupped her full breasts and Kira moaned in ecstasy.

Her nipples were straining against her shirt, visible nubs that gave clear evidence of her lust. His fingers plucked lightly at them, rubbing and tugging alternately until her breath was coming fast.

Unable to stand it any longer, Kira twisted in his arms until she faced him. Her lips grabbed his in total control of a kiss that showed the barely leashed passion inside her. Her tongue duelled with his in a twist of bliss and lust.

As they kissed he worked his hands under her shirt, his fingertips touching her bare skin, gripping her waist in an unmistakably manly gesture. He pulled her against his body and moaned as their lips continued to assault one another.

Swiftly, with desperate need, Michael pulled away long enough to tug her shirt over her head and let it drop to the floor. At the same time Kira was buzzing from the lust she felt and her hands moved to undo the buttons on his shirt, needing to feel skin against skin. Finally the last button gave way and she had his soft body against her needy fingertips. His chest was covered in a light dusting of hair that brushed against her already sensitized flesh.

"My God." Michael moaned as he looked at her breasts, barely encased by the lacy black bra. Her dusky nipples were clearly visible through the material as they stood at attention. "These are perfection." He took both breasts in his hands and leaned over to place urgent kisses on the pale skin that was visible above the bra. Then his lips encircled one of her peaks through the fabric, and Kira groaned as he sucked her nipple into his mouth. The combined pressure of his lips and tongue against the slightly scratchy fabric had Kira gripping his head. His erection pressed against her in a blatant example of his readiness.

His buzz cut felt soft against the skin of her hands as Kira pushed him away from her tortured breasts and pulled his lips back to hers for a fierce kiss. She backed away, forcing Michael to follow her as she moved through the apartment and into her bedroom.

Once inside the soothing, softly lit room Kira pulled away. Her eyes heavy with lust she looked at Michael. His body was even better that she had thought. Well defined muscles, with washboard abs and arms to die for.

For a moment, all her insecurities returned with a blast and she looked away. *Why would such a perfect specimen of man want her, matronly, divorced, and slightly overweight her, when he could have any perfect little perky barely legal woman around?* Her arms moved to automatically hide her waist as she stuttered to a stop, her lust dissolving in a puddle of self-contempt.

"Where'd you go?" Michael moved closer, gripping her hands and forcing them away from her stomach. "Why would you cover this beauty up? Don't hide from me, let me in."

"Why?" Kira mumbled. "I am much too old for you, and you are way too perfect for me." Refusing to give in to the tears that threatened to overwhelm her, Kira blinked rapidly, unable to look at him.

"Bullshit. You are in no way too old for me. I don't care about your age; it's the connection we feel that matters. As to you not being perfect enough for me? I beg to differ." He ran his hands lightly down her arms again. "Your skin is like silk, soft and sensual. Your smile invites me in. Your eyes beg me to make love to you. Your body is a dream—I could lose myself for days just worshipping these beautiful breasts. In a word, you are amazing, woman."

Once again his soothing voice had calmed her nerves and started to rev her engine again. Shaking her head slightly to dislodge any remaining negative thoughts, she sat down on the edge of the bed and smiled at him with one eyebrow cocked, then motioned for him to show her what else he was hiding.

Michael grinned and toed off his shoes in a rush. His fingers worked the button followed by the zipper of his jeans, and slowly slid them down his muscular legs, revealing a pair of black boxer briefs that were straining to contain his erection.

Once again Kira marvelled at his body; she had barely managed to fully acclimate to his well-defined legs when he slid the briefs down his legs and stepped out of them. With trepidation and curiosity (after all, this was only the second penis she would have seen in real life) Kira let her gaze drift up his legs.

She sighed heavily; his Johnson was all that she could have hoped. Thick and long, it stood at attention, bobbing a little in an acknowledgement of her perusal. Unconsciously Kira licked her lips, causing Michael to groan as he moved to the bed.

In bare moments Kira was as naked as Michael; the skinny jeans came off much easier than they went on. Tongues collided, bodies meshed, hands touched as they learned each other's bodies. There was an intensity to Michael as he lavished attention on every inch of Kira's body.

His fingers swept over her mound and with abandon Kira pushed herself up and against his hand. Slowly his fingers rubbed across her burning nub of desire and she groaned, thrashing her head from side to side.

"My God," she stuttered, losing any possible coherent thought as Michael continued the onslaught. He took his time, bringing her repeatedly to the edge of orgasm before backing off, until she thought she would explode from the pure intensity.

"Please, Michael. Please!" she begged, thrusting her pelvis

at his hand, seeking the finish she so desperately craved. With a feral, purely masculine grin, Michael slipped a finger inside her while his thumb pressed firmly against her clitoris, and the world exploded. Kira's orgasm took her by storm, ripping away all sense of equilibrium. Her body became a quivering mass of nerve endings.

She was still in the twitching stage of bliss when she vaguely heard a ripping sound as Michael quickly donned a condom. He parted her legs, positioning himself between her thighs and with barely restrained movements he slowly penetrated her, inch by glorious inch stretching her welcoming warmth with control. His eyes fastened on hers, making sure she stayed on the edge of bliss before he continued. She tilted her pelvis and slipped her legs around his waist so he filled her more deeply than before. With intent, he began to move, slowly at first but steadily increasing in speed and intensity, until he was thrusting into her without restraint.

The angle of his hard body against her soft one pressed her in such a way that she was quickly being brought to orgasm once more. Her eyes widened with shock and pure astonishment; she'd always thought the books and movies made up women having multiple orgasms, but she was thrilled to find out she was wrong, so wrong. He moved inside her like an expert, a *sex*pert who knew exactly how much pressure to use in order to bring the maximum benefit. Her body felt like it was flying, every inch of skin tingling.

Fingers digging into his shoulders, she panted and they moved in perfect time, their sweat-drenched bodies slippery against each other.

His pace increased, and she was caught off guard as another shuddering orgasm snuck up on her. Her insides clenched him tightly, and he gave a primal yell, thrusting into her once more, holding her close as they both rocked from the shattering releases they'd experienced.

Michael collapsed on top of her, somehow managing to keep his weight from smothering her as they tried to catch their breath.

"Kira." Michael moved first, raising himself on his elbows. His hand cupped the side of her face as he whispered. "You are unbelievable."

"You're pretty freaking amazing yourself." Kira's breathing had almost returned to normal when Michael pulled away and disposed of the condom. He returned quickly and pulled her against his hard body.

Kira's exhausted mind tried to put together all that had happened and was unable to. She only knew she felt amazing, wanted, and beautiful. She decided—until later, when she had the energy to analyze everything—that would have to do.

Fitted together, her back to his front in a comfortable and comforting position, they both drifted off to sleep.

5 CHAPTER FIVE

The last few weeks had been an education to Kira. She and Michael fell into a relationship quickly, although they hadn't classified it as such. They spent time together, both in bed and out of it. Michael had an intensity about him; everything he did, he did with passion, as though it was life altering. He never seemed to stop wanting her, and when they were together, he made sure she always took her pleasure first.

Kira's outlook on life, and herself, had greatly altered since her makeover. She noticed she walked with a confidence she'd never had before. While she knew it was an internal shift, having a younger man paying her as much attention as Michael did certainly didn't hurt.

She had come to the realization that although she had been hurt that Steve had left her without attempting to work on their relationship, she wasn't as crushed by it as she should have been. After being with Michael, she looked back at her marriage and saw that the spark had fizzled long before Steve left. She was unable to pinpoint the moment when their passionate kisses had mellowed off to impersonal, punctual pecks. In some ways, Steve had been right to leave her. It took a long time for Kira to accept it, but she no longer loved him either. And although it had been a severe blow to her self-esteem, she knew she was coming out of it a stronger woman.

One night Michael had asked her if he could draw and maybe someday sculpt her. After some argument Kira relented, agreeing to some sketches but no sculpture and no one else could ever see the sketches. Michael had happily played with his sketchbook for several hours while Kira had watched television.

Finally he had revealed a picture of her that was absolutely stunning. His sense of proportion and pure unadulterated talent were amazing. The portrait looked like her, but in a way she'd never seen herself before. It was like looking at herself with someone else's eyes.

After that her confidence had been boosted and she had begun to see that woman, the one with the sparkle in her eyes, in the mirror more and more. She had accepted who she was and no longer did thoughts of unworthiness cloud her thoughts. Or at least not nearly as often; after all, she was still a woman, and all women had doubts. She was proud to have moved on, and Steve's words couldn't hurt her anymore.

They spent time both at Kira's townhouse and at Michael's loft, getting to know one another better and better. Michael needed her in ways she'd never experienced before. He treated her like she was precious and special. He took everything she said seriously, never laughing at her or making her feel like less of a woman for all her lack of ambition. He honestly didn't seem to see any flaw in her. His personality was intense, needy, and she would call it serious, although severe might also describe him. Like most artists, Michael was an all-or-nothing guy. There was no middle ground when it came to his life, art, or opinions.

Kira thought about all of this absently as she brushed her hair, put product in it and fluffed it just as Lindsay had shown her. She looked in the mirror and grinned; so much change in such a short time.

The doorbell rang and Kira grabbed her bag as she whipped out of the room. Tonight they were going out, the first time since they had gotten together. For the last two weeks it had been sexfest 2014—they had barely left the bedroom, let alone gone out to socialize.

Kira yanked open the door and grinned at Michael, who—as always—looked scrumptious in a red fitted button-down shirt and hip-hugging black jeans.

Michael leaned in to give her a kiss. When their lips touched, the passion that was always just below the surface fluttered to life. Regretfully Kira pulled away first, determined not to get dragged in by the unmistakeable lust she felt filling her loins.

"You look beautiful." Michael said.

"Thanks." Kira had carefully chosen a short black dress from her closet. It had a flared waist and showed off her long legs to maximum benefit. The top was fitted with a modestly cut bust line, showing some cleavage without seeming sleazy. On her feet was a new pair of black platform pumps with four-inch heels. In these shoes she stood taller than Michael, but he didn't care.

"Are you sure we have to go out?" Michael moaned. He cupped his hands behind her back, pulling her close. "We could just head back into your bedroom and I could show you how great you look." His eyes shone with longing.

Kira laughed and pulled away. "Nice try. I want to go out for dinner, I start my new job tomorrow and I want to celebrate. It also feels like we've been shipwrecked here, never seeing anyone. Just living for the next time we have sex."

"We saw the pizza delivery man just last night." Michael's face was serious.

"Okay, I'll give you that. I'm just feeling closeted. I need to go out."

"Alright." Michael seemed slightly disappointed. But he agreed to her request without any further complaint.

Kira led the way out of her apartment and to her car. Wearing a skirt made the motorcycle out of the question for tonight, so she was happy to drive.

They made their way across town; in mutual agreement they had decided to go to Dominic's. In Chatelane there weren't many choices of restaurants, let alone good ones.

Since they both liked Dominic's, it was an easy decision.

Kira pulled into a spot with ease, and carefully (so as to not flash anyone her vajayjay) got out of the car. Michael put his hand on her lower back and the two of them went into the restaurant.

Inside, the warm colours and soothing atmosphere put her at ease immediately. They stepped up to the hostess stand, where a middle-aged woman waited.

"Table for two?" she asked with a practiced, impersonal glance.

"Actually," Kira smiled, "I think we'd like to sit at the family table. Thank you."

The hostess nodded and led them through the restaurant to the table, where four other people already sat. As she approached, Kira noticed a few looks from men, who stared unabashedly at her legs. She ducked her eyes self-consciously. Then, frowning inwardly, she decided to enjoy the moment. With a smile she raised her face and basked in the attention.

Michael pulled out her chair and sat beside her. Across from them was an older gentleman who was having a lively discussion with a young woman. Beside them was another couple in their mid-twenties who sat across from each other.

Once the conversation came to a natural lull, Kira introduced herself. "Hi, I'm Kira and this is Michael." She waved a hand indicating they were together.

"I'm Will." The older gentleman spoke with a grin and reached a hand across to shake their hands. He directed a harmless grin at Michael and added, "You sure lucked out with this knockout." He tilted his head at Kira, his lively blue eyes twinkling. "I noticed her coming from across the room—a tall drink of cold water this one is."

Kira blushed and thanked Will for the compliment.

The young woman sitting beside Will smiled at them. For some reason the smile unnerved Kira, as it somehow didn't connect with her eyes. "I'm Sharon." Her long blonde hair was pulled up in an artfully messy bun on the top of her head.

Her petite face was tanned and well made up. The understated diamond studs in her ears and matching tennis bracelet showed her to be better off than most.

The couple at the end of the table introduced themselves as Jeff and Tracy. They seemed like a nice couple, always smiling at each other and holding hands across the table. They gave a simultaneous head nod to greet the additions to the table. As though it was a natural thing, the conversation started back up with ease.

The discussion had just turned to weather when the waiter, a balding man with a thin moustache came to take orders. His expression was grim, and his cheekbones stood out in a way that made his eyes appear sunken. He looked like he should be a sourpuss, but he actually turned out to be quite friendly, and when he smiled the severity of his face disappeared.

After the waiter brought them drinks, Jeff was telling the story of how he and Tracy had met when a throat was cleared from behind Kira.

She turned and her heart leapt when she saw Dom. He looked good, dressed in a crisp yellow high-necked button-down shirt that showed off his olive skin tone, paired with perfectly pleated black dress pants. His shaggy hair hung over his forehead as though he had just run his fingers through it. She smiled; even if he was a married man, he was a good friend and she hated how they had left things so angry the last time they had seen one another.

She stood and hugged Dom, whispering, "I am sorry. I was a total bitch last time I was here. Please forgive me."

Dom returned her hug enthusiastically. "No, I'm the one who is sorry. I should have been more supportive, and less judgemental of you. You shocked me, is all."

He held her away from him, looking into her eyes and speaking loud enough for the entire table to hear. "Kira, you look lovely. I am absolutely thrilled you decided to come to Dominic's tonight."

He turned to the rest of the table, his accent becoming

more pronounced as he said, "I trust everything is perfection at the family table tonight?" Nods all around the table greeted his proclamation.

"Perfetto." Dom grinned. "Let me know if I can be of further service."

He gave a little half bow that didn't look nearly as stupid as it should have and turned back to Kira, his blue eyes twinkling with pure joy. "I may join you later for a drink. Then we can catch up."

"That would be very nice." Kira replied happily. Dom, the consummate gentleman, pulled her chair out and helped her return to her seat before he disappeared behind the bar.

She turned back to the table. "That was Dom. He owns the place," she explained.

Sharon leaned her chin on her hand and snarkily said, "Dom, huh? It seems like you two were awfully close."

Kira laughed. "It's not like that. Dom is a friend, a married friend at that."

Will cleared his throat and mumbled. "Married or not, the way he was looking at you tells me he wishes it was more than friendship."

Sharon nodded, and her eyes slid to Michael to see his reaction as she added, "His eyes were on your legs the whole time." Sharon's eyes were mean as she riled the table up further with her innuendos.

"It's really not like that." Kira protested. "I'm dating Michael."

"Uh-huh." Even Jeff seemed unsure.

Sharon's eyes feasted on Michael as though he was a lobster dinner. "Me thinks thou doth protest too much." She giggled lightly, trying to make her comments seem like harmless teasing rather than the blatant attempt at boyfriend hijacking that they obviously were.

Kira was saved from having to defend herself any further when their food arrived. She looked at Michael, relieved to see him look so relaxed. She reached out and squeezed his hand; he looked in her eyes and smiled lightly. The secret smile of a lover, which made Kira's insides stand up and sing.

"You okay?" she whispered.

"Fine." His thumb rubbed the back of her hand lightly. "They can say what they want. I'm secure enough in my manhood to not worry. Besides, having other men lust after you is a real plus, because I know you're coming home with me."

After dinner was consumed, the table was loudly debating a local politician's ability when Dom reappeared.

"Anyone mind if I join you for a while?" he asked, to which everyone concurred, and Dom sat across from Michael.

"Everyone, this is Dom." Kira announced. "Dom, this is Will, Sharon, Jeff, Tracy and this is Michael." She waved her hand at each person in turn, making sure the introductions were complete.

"Pleasure to meet all of you. Please continue your conversation."

Will took the conversational reins and continued on his rant about infrastructure and the mayoral position.

Kira was never one to follow politics, whether they were municipal, provincial, or federal, so she just sat back with her glass of wine and watched the debate grow semi heated. Dom brought in a new perspective as a business owner and the challenges faced strictly by businesses. Will brought the old-boys-club mentality. Jeff and Tracy were united in their beliefs about sustainability and the new way to do things, while Sharon brought the privileged attitude of someone who had never worked a day in their lives. Michael was the group's lone artist and he espoused the need for more arts programs and support.

The political conversation turned into a debate about climate change, then to history, and so on. It morphed and shaped itself based on statements made. Like a growing child, the conversation took on a life of its own, growing in length and changing in unexpected ways. Kira was the observer; when she had an opinion she voiced it, but in general she found just listening was enough for her.

Overall it was a pleasant way to spend the evening. None of the table's inhabitants got so upset they were angry, but it was a lively conversation full of arm gestures, raised voices and even laughter.

Occasionally Michael's hand would stray below the table and rest lightly on her bare thigh. His soft, knowing fingers would stroke her skin until she clenched her jaw. Just as she was about to explode he would remove his hand, with no one at the table any wiser. All night he kept her on edge, knowing exactly how far to take it without going too far. He could tell by the way she moved how much he was turning her on, and when to stop. He never actually reached under the hem of her skirt, but just his touch on her was enough to set her blood boiling and her libido galloping.

Eventually Jeff looked at his watch and jumped. "Holy God, it's nearly eleven o'clock. We need to be getting home."

That seemed to be the signal for the table to break up, with everyone saying their good-byes and paying bills. Michael sat with his arm around Kira as they thanked everyone for the great conversation and company. Dom made his way into the kitchen to check on some detail with the sous chef.

"Would you like to dance?" Michael turned towards Kira, his hand held out.

"Michael, no one else is dancing." Kira said self-consciously.

"Then we will be the first and set the standard. I won't take no for an answer." He stood, pulling Kira to her feet and walking towards the small dance floor. The music was low, a background sound, but Kira could make out the dulcet tones of John Legend as he sang "All of Me."

Almost before she knew it, Michael had wrapped his strong hands around her waist and started to sway to the music. As always when Michael was close to her, her pulse began to race. She leaned in and placed her cheek against his, listening to him as he sang the lyrics in a low, surprisingly in-tune, pleasant baritone.

"Love your curves and all your edges, your perfect imperfections, give your all to me, I'll give my all to you. You're my end and my beginning, even when I lose I'm winning, cause I give you all of me, and you give me all of you."

Kira closed her eyes and enjoyed the pleasant sound of his voice, the whisper in her ear, his hard body pressed against hers. She found herself thinking about the song, and what it meant.

Who do I want to sing that song to? I like Michael, he's intense, exciting, ever so good in bed, and he needs me. The attraction between us is undeniable. But do I want to give "all of me" to him? Or for that matter any man? After giving everything to Steve, was she gun-shy about the dreaded "L" word?

Before her thoughts could stray any further into unwanted territory, she reminded herself it was too early in their relationship for these types of thoughts. In her mind, they didn't know each other well enough to make that decision or to even worry about it yet.

She opened her eyes and a movement from across the room drew her attention. Dom stood, half in shadows, staring at the dance floor with what appeared to be a sad look on his face. Before she could look further to decipher his thoughts, he disappeared into the kitchen.

"You were right." Michael whispered in her ear, distracting her from her worries about Dom. "We needed to get out. I liked showing you off to the world. And I must add your legs look absolutely hot in that dress. Thank you for pushing me about it."

"You're welcome." Kira's lips curved into a soft smile. He moved slightly, but deliberately, placing his muscular thigh directly between her legs, pressing intimately against her pelvis. The heat from his body infiltrated her blood, and she felt a familiar pulsing below her belly button start. She drew a sharp breath, and her eyes flew to his, as the friction of their movements brought him to rub directly on her always sensitive clit.

"So, have we had enough of being in public?" He grinned as Kira nodded, mutely. That's good because I need to get you home, naked, and underneath me. Or overtop of me—your call."

They paid their bill and made their way out to the car quickly. Dom hadn't come back out of the kitchen, so she had been unable to say good-bye to him. As she got in the car, she felt a twinge of regret, which was soon forgotten as Michael placed his hand once more on her thigh. This time he ventured above the hemline.

6 CHAPTER SIX

A few weeks later Kira was beginning to feel comfortable with her new job. She had started at the local newspaper, The Chatelane *Herald*, as a receptionist. It wasn't a glamorous job, but she felt useful and independent for the first time in many years. No one here knew the old Kira; they took her at face value. There were even a couple of people she had met that she could see becoming good friends with in the future.

That was one thing she mourned about the end of her marriage: all the mutual friends they had had went with Steve. The only exception had been her close friend from high school, who unfortunately had moved to Vancouver a few years ago. So although Tracy was incredibly supportive, she lived three thousand miles away, making pity drinks hard to accomplish. They stayed in contact regularly, but it wasn't the same.

At the time, when she'd realized all the women she considered close were only close because of Steve, she had been crushed. However, she had decided if that was their choice, well, they obviously weren't good friends anyway. Now she was moving on, developing relationships, making connections, being alive.

Overall she was happy as she pulled into the parking lot of Michael's building. He lived above a shop in downtown Chatelane, in a loft-style apartment. It was open concept, serving as both his studio and as his living space. The space was mostly unfinished with bare walls and exposed ceiling beams; however the sixteen-foot ceilings and large windows allowed an abundance of light in and gave it a New York, bohemian style that Kira appreciated.

There was a small kitchenette in one corner; with a bar fridge and micro stove that served Michael well enough. The living space was right beside that and consisted of a futon couch and lots of shelves stuffed full of books. Michael had no television, claiming he would rather read or create than be forced to view the inferior creations of others. At times Kira missed the television, watching movies while cuddling on the couch. Or gapping out on *Say Yes to the Dress*, but she could always watch at home, and she PVRed everything good anyway.

The bathroom was barely a closet and held only the toilet and a sink. The claw foot tub was located in the main room, between the bedroom and living room. The first time Michael had run her a bath had been liberating and incredibly sensual; the idea had at first terrified her but eventually she came to love the freedom. After the bath they had had unbelievably hot sex on top of the work bench.

The bedroom was located on the back wall, centered around a huge bed with a sculpted headboard that rose eight feet above them and surrounded the entire king-sized bed. Michael had made it to resemble a wave crashing into rocks; the mattress looked like it was floating on water. It was a piece that denied its medium. At first glance it looked like it was carved from stone, and only upon closer examination was Kira able to tell that it was actually wood. This piece, more than any picture, had convinced Kira of Michael's pure, untainted talent.

Seventy percent of the loft was taken over by Michael's studio. It stood close to the windows, capitalizing on the natural light. He had all sorts of carving tools, chunks of wood ranging in size from one foot square to ones that were five or six feet across, a chainsaw, cutting tools and all manner of other assorted thingamabobs.

He was slowly but surely developing a name within the art community, having completed sculptures for many big businesses and individual commissions as well. A Toronto gallery had recently contacted him about hosting an art show six months from now. It was sure to catapult his career.

There were many projects dotting the space, each in various stages of completion, some covered with large drop sheets and others visible. This allowed Michael to work easily on one piece or another and not be distracted. Michael claimed to have lucked out finding a place this size that also had a freight elevator for moving all his projects in and out.

Kira buzzed at the back door and waited for Michael to open the security lock. Eventually he buzzed her in with a distracted "Come up." She walked through the old loading dock, got in the elevator and pulled the safety gate down behind her. Hitting the large black button to the left of the door, the lift slowly began its ascent.

She barely refrained from tapping her foot impatiently. The elevator was old and clunky and took what seemed like forever to reach the second floor. Unfortunately the only stair access would be classified as more of a ladder, and Kira would only use it in cases of extreme emergency, like the building was on fire or collapsing.

Finally the lift rose above the floor of the upper level, and as it elevated further, Kira could see more and more of the room. Michael was working away in the studio, which was odd; normally he finished by the time she was done work so they could spend time together.

She toed off her high heels, with a sigh of pure bliss at the flattening of her arches, then, dropping her purse on the counter, she slipped towards the studio.

At the sound off her approach Michael turned, a huge grin on his face. He was in front of a project that was normally covered and he rushed towards Kira, pulling her in for a wet kiss that was more habitual than erotic. Nonetheless, the mere brushing of his lips against hers was enough to set her libido galloping.

"How was work?" he asked distractedly.

"Pretty good, I'm glad it's Friday though. You look like

you've had a good day." Kira answered.

"I did. Actually I had a great day." Michael grinned infectiously; his happiness was like a kid on Christmas, making it impossible for Kira to not smile back as he continued. "I want to show you a piece I've been working on. I started it a couple weeks ago, and it has really come together the last few days. It still needs final touches and stain, but I sent a few shots of it to some of my buyers and I've already gotten offers on it."

"Wow that's great Michael. Offers on unfinished work—has that ever happened before?"

"Nope." He grinned again. "Wait till you see it."

Michael grabbed her hand and pulled her along to where he was working when she came in. He stood in front of a large piece that Kira couldn't see around his large body, as he turned to face her. "I want to see your reaction," he said, and then stepped quickly to the side.

She gasped and covered her mouth with her hand, unsure how to react. She faced a larger-than-life sculpture of herself, rising from a series of flames that obscured the bottom half of her body slightly. One of her long legs stepped gracefully from the fire, toes pointed, but the flames did cover her hoo-ha somewhat. From the waist up she was naked as the day she was born. Her head was thrown back in what was obviously Kira's ecstasy face, her hands buried in her hair.

The art-appreciating side of Kira wanted to admire the skill that had obviously gone into such a piece. The wood looked soft where it was her body, and translated a sense of movement through the flames; it was beautifully done. However, the part of her that was Kira was mortified; truly horrified that Michael would sculpt her when she had explicitly asked him not to. It only made it worse that it was a naked sculpture of her in the throes of passion. The expression on her face was one that should only be seen inside a bedroom.

She was unable to talk as she stared at her own face. The grain of the wood made it look like she had tears running down her cheeks, the parted mouth looked realistic enough to speak. Every detail of her body, from the indented scar on her left arm to the mole under her left breast was sculpted perfectly. It was as though she was a victim of a variant version of Medusa, one whose gaze turned living flesh into solid wood.

"I…." And words failed her.

"Isn't it fabulous?" Michael seemed oblivious to Kira's discomfort. "It was so hard to get the texture right, especially here." Michael's hands ran lightly over the slightly pouched stomach of the sculpted Kira. "And here." He cupped the breast lightly. "But I did it. It's my masterpiece."

"I…." Kira tried again and still was unable to speak.

"Kira, love, talk to me. Tell me what you think." While he turned towards Kira, his fingers continued to caress the wooden sculpture in a disconcerting way.

She suddenly remembered Michael had shown this piece to several buyers already, and anger like she'd never felt before boiled to the surface, but she fought to retain her calm. "I can't believe you did this to me. I told you not to sculpt me."

"Yeah, but you didn't mean it." Michael turned back to the sculpture, his eyes going soft as he lightly ran his fingers over the wood surface.

"No. I really did mean it." Her voice snapped, his eyes flying back to hers. "I meant it. And for god's sakes, will you stop touching it!" she yelled. Shocked, he dropped his hand to his side, fingers still twitching. Kira ignored them and continued. "The piece is beautiful, but you can't sell it. It's disturbing, why would you put my orgasm face on it?"

"Because that's when you are most beautiful, the moment you are released from the bonds of propriety and let yourself go." Michael stepped towards Kira, who held up her hands, keeping him at bay.

"You can't sell it. I can't have people looking at me, seeing me like this."

"Of course I have to sell it. I've already been offered ten

thousand dollars for this piece alone. That's more than I've ever been paid for a sculpture." Michael's eyes showed his shock at the thought.

"Fine, but change the face. Make it someone else. Not me." Kira crossed her arms over her chest.

"No!" Michael erupted. "The piece is nothing if it isn't you. I can't just 'change the face'. My God, you are being childish."

"Childish?" Kira yelled back, her anger coming undone from the tightly woven coil she had tried to confine it to. "You didn't have any right to create a naked sculpture of me, without my permission! Let alone do it and show it around for the amusement of you and your friends! I won't let you sell it."

"You can't stop me!" Michael yelled back. "It's my art. I have the right to sell it as I wish. Most women are honoured to have the privilege of being an artist's muse. I don't understand you!" He threw up his hands and turned his back, as though dismissing her and her concerns.

Kira's anger went from red hot to ice cold. She hated being dismissed. As he turned she noticed the tag on the bottom of the piece; carved into the flames were the words, *Kira's Ecstasy*. It was the last straw.

"If you dare sell that piece, I will sue you. You do not have my permission, either explicit or implied, to use my likeness. Trust me, Michael; I learned a lot from watching Judge Judy. Sell it and you'll pay."

"So what the hell am I supposed to do with it then?" he yelled back, whipping around at her cold tone.

"I don't care, but you can't put it on display, you can't use it, you can't sell it. It is a perfect likeness of your lover— maybe you should keep it for yourself. Some things, like *My Ecstasy*, are meant to be private! I shared that with you and you alone—not for any Tom, Dick, or Harry to see."

"I was inspired by your beauty and my emotions for you. I have to share those with the world. Kira, please. It truly is my masterpiece. The best piece of work I've ever done." His voice was certain as he looked at her. "You won't sue me."

"Try me. Michael, I assure you, I will sue you. I will. Do you not see why I am upset? You've turned me into a prostitute!"

"That's ridiculous." he snapped, his brown eyes rolling at the suggestion.

"Really? So my image, a piece of me, is going to be sold. Maybe be in a gallery, where a multitude of people will pay to see me naked. How the hell is that not prostitution? Or at the very least the equivalent to being a stripper? Either way, I am neither of those things, nor do I care to be!"

"That's simply not true." He shook his head and continued. "Please Kira, just think about it. Let the idea sink in—it was wrong of me to spring it on you like this. Give it time, you'll get used to the idea." His voice was pleading.

"I won't change my mind. No amount of time could make me change my mind. I can't believe you did this to me." Kira was mortified to feel tears filling her eyes and she furiously scrubbed them away. "I truly cared for you and you betrayed my trust. You're an asshole."

Unable to look at the piece or him any longer, Kira turned on her heel and stormed across the room, grabbing her purse and shoes and throwing herself into the elevator.

The lift began its laborious descent and through the slats of the security gate, she could see Michael's forlorn face as he stared at the wooden Kira.

7 CHAPTER SEVEN

Kira felt the world come into reality as she swam her way to consciousness. Her head was pounding and her mouth felt like she had swallowed fifty-grit sandpaper. She refused to open her eyes, knowing the sharp agony that would bring.

Maybe if I just lie here long enough the pain will go away. I'll keep my eyes closed against the light and the world will be fine, she thought softly.

As she waited for the throbbing to dull, she went over what she remembered from the night before. After she had left Michael's, the foremost thought in her brain was that alcohol had to help. She remembered visiting, and being kicked out of all four of the bars in Chatelane.

At the first bar, The Hangout, after her fourth shot, she had started arguing with some young chick that butted in line ahead of her. It hadn't come to blows, but it was a close thing. Ejection number one.

Then she had proceeded to Donovan's Irish Pub, and after only three drinks there been politely asked to leave by the beefy bouncer. She hadn't known it was against policy to jump on tables and politely ask everyone's opinion about her predicament with Michael.

The third bar, The Terrace, a high-class blues bar, had asked her to leave after her first drink when she had begun singing along with the live band, rather loudly and out of tune. Kira mentally cringed as she remembered the singing.

At the final location, Hijinks, a dance bar frequented by young college students, she was ejected before she'd managed to have a full drink. It wasn't her fault that people had stepped in front of her, causing her to spill her drink all over them. Twice. She had apologized, but that wasn't good enough for the management of the bar and she had been kicked out of that one too.

As she had exited Hijinks she remembered noticing how close she was to Dominic's and thought maybe Dom would share one drink, or four, with her. So, taking off her heels, she had stumbled barefoot the block and a half to her favourite restaurant.

With some dismay, Kira realized that after arriving at Dominic's her memory started to get fuzzy. Fuzzy as in she couldn't remember anything. She pushed her tortured brain to the limit but nothing sparked beyond her walking through Dominic's door and asking Billy, the bartender, for a drink.

Distressed, Kira moved slightly, her hand brushing against the crisp cotton linens and she froze. Her bed did not have cotton sheets; the air conditioning in the townhouse kept her bedroom cooler than she preferred and she had bought thick flannel sheets to keep her warm.

Slowly, confused, she allowed her eyes to flutter open. Blinking rapidly at the invading light, Kira tried to make the world come into focus. A large room that was not her own assaulted her senses. The walls were a pale blue, the king sized bed she lay on covered in top-of-the-line, soft cotton sheets. A large circular window covered only in a sheer, pleated blind allowed diffused, but still painful, light in to flood the room.

She sat up, immediately pressing her hand to her head, groaning as she tried to hold her brains in. Her other hand clutched the blankets to her chest; she was terrified to look and see if she was naked beneath. Pushing back both the pain and the fear, she peeked under the heavy comforter, shocked to see that she wore only her skimpy bra and thong. With no memory of how she had come to be here or what she had done, Kira vowed never to drink again. At thirty-eight she'd never had to take the walk of shame, but it looked like today was going to be the first.

She glanced around, desperately looking for her clothes when a noise caught her attention. Alerted, Kira watched as the door to the room slowly opened, her heart thumping louder than the pounding still rebounding inside her head.

"Kira?" a voice whispered. "Are you awake?"

"Uh-huh." Kira clutched the blanket tighter as she affirmed that she was indeed awake, even though she was internally begging for this to be a nightmare. Unfortunately for Kira and her hopes of unconsciousness, the door swung open slowly. She held her breath, waiting to see what kind of psychopath came through the door.

"Good morning." And in walked Dom. Kira gasped with relief at not finding herself at the mercy of some serial rapist.

"Dom!" she exclaimed, and then winced at the loudness of her own voice.

"I bet your head is not feeling so happy right now, *cara*." Dom leaned casually against the doorframe, a smile softly playing on his lips.

"God no." Kira moaned, to which Dom laughed lightly.

"Listen, there's a shower in there." He waved a hand towards another door off the main room. "Feel free to use it and the bathrobe in there. Your clothes from last night are in the drier. You appear to have spilt some alcohol on them, so I threw them in to wash last night. When you're done, come on downstairs, I'll have some breakfast waiting."

"Okay." Kira felt much better knowing she had not gone home with a complete stranger. Dom left the room on silent feet, pulling the door closed behind him.

Pushing all thoughts besides feeling better out of her mind, Kira stumbled across the room and into the en suite. Barely noticing the beauty of the designer room, she focused on getting into the shower and feeling somewhat more human.

Twenty minutes later, Kira finger combed her damp hair back from her face. Her head was only throbbing enough to stop a freight train, but she felt much better. Dom had thoughtfully left an unopened toothbrush on the counter so her mouth no longer felt, or smelt, like something had died in there. Thus prepared, she pulled the tie tight on the dark blue terry cloth robe and exited the bedroom.

Outside the door she looked over a railing and down to a living room area. An open style staircase led down to the main floor, where she could hear movement.

As she walked down the stairs, Kira took note of the living room. It was a two-storey room, boasting a huge sectional sofa on one end, which faced a flagstone fireplace complete with large television mounted above. One entire wall was floor to ceiling windows that looked out over the river and parkland surrounding. She walked across the thick carpeting, her toes sinking into the softness as she approached the kitchen cautiously.

She looked through the wide archway, appreciating the dark wood cabinets, the pale granite counters, and ceramic flooring tiles. The room was huge, with a breakfast nook that looked out on a very pretty little garden.

Dom had his back to her as he worked away at the stove located in the center island. Delicious scents wafted through the air, assaulting Kira's nose. The smell of bacon should have turned her stomach, but instead made her stomach rumble.

She cleared her throat and Dom turned with a big smile on his face. "Hey. How are you feeling now?"

"I think I'll live." Kira advanced into the room and Dom motioned her to sit at the table, handing her a coffee as she passed him.

"I am glad to hear it. Breakfast is just about ready," he said.

Kira sat, carefully arranging the robe so that it covered as much of her legs as possible. She blew on the coffee and sipped carefully on the heavenly brew.

"So." Kira started. "I, um, seem to have gotten pretty zambonied last night and don't exactly remember everything that happened."

To her annoyance, Dom laughed. "That doesn't surprise me. You were as drunk as I have ever seen you."

"Okay. Fine. Laugh at me." Kira huffed, and then she got going and began to ramble. "Just answer my questions, tell me the truth. How the hell did I end up in your bed? And almost naked? Did I talk to you about what happened with Michael? Did I do anything embarrassing? Did we?" Dom looked at her with an almost visible question mark above his head. "Well, did we do 'it'? You know, 'the nasty,' 'the deed,' 'the horizontal mambo—did we have sex? And where is your wife and what will she think?"

Silence took over the room for a few moments while Dom plated the bacon and eggs, then came over and handed Kira her breakfast. He sat down slowly and took his coffee in hand.

"Why don't I tell you what happened, and afterwards you can ask any questions to fill in what I may miss from the story?"

Kira thought about it, and then nodded in agreement.

"You should eat while I talk. Your body needs the nutrients after last night. *Mangiare! Mangiare!*" Dom smiled again and motioned at her plate as he began to talk.

"Last night, around eleven, you came into the restaurant. You appeared as intoxicated as the proverbial village drunk. Billy served you a virgin drink—without you knowing, I might add—and then called me to the front. When I came in, you were, well, very friendly." He looked at Kira, his blue eyes piercing as he smiled at her. "Don't worry. I don't believe in taking advantage of inebriated women. You cried on my shoulder about what that douche puppet Michael did. You were very distraught. I wouldn't say embarrassing, per se. But obviously upset."

Dom paused and took a sip of his coffee; then, setting his cup to the side, he steepled his fingers in front of him and continued. "Once the bar had closed, you were in bad shape indeed. I brought you back here, as a friend, so I could take care of you. Once we arrived, you got a spurt of energy and stripped yourself down to your…"—he cleared his throat—"very attractive, very tiny unmentionables. And climbed into my bed. I will be honest. You did, sort of, beg me to make love to you. But as I said, I don't take advantage of drunken women. No matter how appealing the offer might be."

Kira dropped her eyes, horrified that she had thrown herself at Dom. "I'm sorry. I stripped in front of you? And begged you?" she mumbled.

"You did attempt a strip tease, of sorts. It might have been quite sexy if you weren't falling over drunk. And yes, you did ask, repeatedly, for me to come to bed with you but it is okay, you were out of your mind." Dom smiled.

"It's not acceptable," Kira moaned, full of distress. "I have never thrown myself at anyone. I cannot believe I acted like such a fool. I am so sorry."

"Don't think about it. We all do foolish things when we are drunk. You just experienced your coming of age moment later than most. Now let me continue—you interrupted before I was finished," Dom chided her gently. "I believe your final questions were in regards to my wife. I have wanted to tell you for some time that I don't have a wife anymore. The ring you saw was indeed my wedding ring, but I honestly forgot I still wore it. It had become a habit, one that I had no idea I had. And I had no idea you assumed I was still wed until the night of your makeover."

"So where is your wife?" Kira asked quietly, the shock of Dom not being married almost jolting her out of the hangover.

"It's a rather long story." Dom looked down at his long fingers as they held his coffee.

"I've got the time," Kira said with a smile, and then continued in a more serious voice. "Please, you've listened to all my woes and problems and never told me about you. I feel like a bad friend. Tell me about your wife. Let me be the one you talk to for once."

"All right." Dom sat back in his chair, lost in thought. His eyes looked out the window as he chose his wording.

Kira held her breath in the silence, hoping that he wouldn't change his mind; he swung his piercing blue eyes to meet hers and finally spoke.

"I married Jennifer right out of college. It was a deep and true love. She was everything a good Italian wants for a wife: beautiful, a good cook, full of laughter, great in bed, and she wanted kids right away. To say she was my everything is an understatement. As I started Dominic's, Jennifer set about making our family life exactly what we'd always discussed. But for some reason she never got pregnant. We tried for a number of years. I was too stubborn to get help. That and, in my defence, I was busy getting the restaurant up and going." He paused, lost in memories of a life left behind.

"Three years after we were married, I finally agreed to get medical help. What had at first seemed like an unnecessary intrusion into our lives had started to concern me. Truly, with three years of trying, in my mind, we should have had some result, some pregnancy, something. After a battery of tests, we finally got answers. Jennifer had a tumour the size of an orange inside her uterus. Inoperable. Terminal. The cancer was too far gone. For a year we ignored the worst-case scenario and tried chemotherapy, radiation therapy, and everything I could think of.

"My brother, Nico, came over from Italy and ran the restaurant for me while I cared for Jennifer. She became my sole focus. In that year, I watched her fade. She went from beautiful and vibrant and full of life, to a shell, a mere shadow of the woman she had been. The medicines didn't help. Nothing I did helped her. Nothing I did could save her. She still died."

He looked at Kira, his eyes sad. "She was twenty-five years old, as was I. A twenty-five-year-old widower who thought his life had ended when his wife died. That was almost twenty years ago. I mourned for a long time. There is a period of almost a year I don't remember. I did nothing but sit and rail at the fates for taking her from me. I hated life, I hated God, and I even began to hate Jennifer, thinking she had given up. But more than anything I hated myself. If only I'd gotten tested sooner, maybe we could have caught the cancer early enough to save her. My family and friends drifted away. They felt sorry for me but couldn't stand to be near me and my seemingly endless state of mourning any longer." His voice faded and silence enveloped them for a few minutes until Dom cleared his throat and spoke quietly.

"Even a grief as deep as mine was fades. There came a day when I smiled, and laughed, and eventually the days where I was happy outnumbered the ones where I couldn't breathe for the pain. I've come to accept that I can remember and love my first wife and still move on. It's what Jennifer would have wanted. She would never have wanted me to spend twenty years alone, living a half-life."

"I am so sorry, Dom," Kira whispered, her eyes filled with tears at his heart-wrenching story.

"I do not tell you now to look for your pity, but so that you can understand why I still wore my ring. Not because I still mourned my wife, or because I am still married to her, or her memory. But rather because it was a habit." Dom looked away as he spoke.

"I've been ready to move on for a number of years, but I never found anyone I thought about in a romantic way. I had given up hope of there being another woman for me. There was no one who made my heart sing like my Jennifer did. Then, almost a year ago, you stumbled into my restaurant and my life. I'd finally found someone who would make me risk my heart again. But, you were too angry, so hurt by your ex. You needed to heal. So I became your friend, which I have never regretted. I had hoped when the time came and you were ready, that you would turn to me and we could take our friendship to something more, but it didn't work out that way." He smiled sadly.

"Dom, I—" Kira began, but he waved her into silence.

"Please, Kira let me finish. You are perfect, as you are now and as you were before your makeover. I love the way your eyes crinkle when you laugh, I love your opinions, your laugh, the way that you have to finish each piece of food one at a time before you can move on to the next item on your plate. I love the colour of your hair, the beautiful, unbelievable legs that you possess, your morals, your sense of humour. I want nothing more than for you to give me a chance to be the man that you need."

Kira's brain was swimming, and from more than just the hangover now. "I am at a loss," she whispered, looking into Dom's eyes, the eyes of her friend, and wanted nothing more than to give him the chance he asked for. "But—I am dating Michael."

"I know," Dom said sadly, his barely perceptible accent softly caressing her ears. "I know you aren't the type of woman to step out on her boyfriend. However, I also believe Michael has overstepped and stretched your trust, so perhaps the entire relationship needs re-evaluating. I just ask that you think of me as an option when you are debating your status with him."

"Okay." Kira smiled softly. "I will."

"I also ask that before you decide you give each of us a chance and offer me some equal time." Dom leaned towards Kira, his hand grasping hers.

"What do you mean by that?" Kira tilted her head as she evaluated him.

"Just that Michael has had more of a chance to stand out on a romantic level than I, simply by being in a romantic relationship rather than a friendly one. So I would ask that you consent to go on a date or two with me before making your final decision." He smiled broadly and Kira felt her insides quiver at the pure masculinity in his face.

"Alright. One date. Then I'll talk to Michael and make a choice." Kira squeezed his hand, glad of the firm pressure.

"Tonight?"

Kira took a deep breath. "You know how far outside my comfort level you are putting me, don't you?" Dom nodded. "I'm not the type of woman to date two men at the same time."

"We've already established that, Kira. You aren't dating two men at once; you are going on a date with another man. It's a fine distinction, but a clear one nonetheless. So, tonight?" His accent became more pronounced as he spoke.

Kira simply nodded. "Pick me up at eight?"

"Better make it seven." Dom grinned happily.

.

8 CHAPTER EIGHT

At seven Kira was wandering aimlessly around her apartment, her nerves overwhelming her. All day the guilt she felt towards Michael had been at the forefront of her mind. It didn't help that he had texted her several dozen times, all apologetic. Excluding the fact that she was going on a date tonight, she was still too hurt and angry to respond. There had been however, quite a few moments where she had almost cancelled on Dom. All day she had bandied the idea back and forth, almost cancelling, and then changing her mind again and again. Something stopped her though; they got along so well that she just couldn't make herself back out. She didn't *want* to back out.

She wandered around her apartment, absentmindedly picking up knickknacks, then putting them back down. She found it impossible to sit still; the inner turmoil she felt still volleyed around in her mind. She shook her head. It was Dom. Dom. She didn't understand the nervous energy. She had always found him incredibly attractive, and they were such great friends that she knew her anxiety was a result of the guilt she felt towards Michael. As well as worry about the repercussions to her friendship with Dom.

The truth was she wanted to go out with Dom, to see what it was like to go on a date with him. Her inner rebel was screaming at her to just do it, to live, to experience life. She had been married for so long, and had never really had a chance to be a young single woman kicking ass and taking names. This was her chance.

She kept telling herself that she and Michael had never promised exclusivity, and that assuaged her self-condemnation, somewhat.

She checked the mirror beside the front door again. The text she had received from Dom told her to dress casual. She wore a pair of dark blue jeans paired with calf-high black boots that were reminiscent of Doc Martens. She tugged on the fitted blue tank top she wore layered under a black one, trying to make sure they covered her stomach enough while still not baring all of her cleavage. It was a delicate balance that she often messed up. Once she was satisfied that her clothes passed the bill as well as could be expected, she turned to fuss with her styled hair, and the light almost nonexistent makeup she wore. She only hoped he had meant it when he said casual.

The doorbell rang, causing Kira to jump at the sudden intrusion. Giggling at herself, she smoothed a hand over her hair a final time and turned to the door, opening it with a smile.

Dom stood on the other side, a smile lighting his eyes as he looked at Kira.

"Hey," Kira mumbled awkwardly. Dom looked good enough to eat, his black jeans molded to legs that were long, with well-defined muscles. He wore a simple black T-shirt that showed evidence of his familiarity with a gym. Where Michael was bulky muscles and a body-building frame, Dom was lean masculinity. Each muscle group was defined without being overbuilt. His strength was understated. Kira smiled shyly, unsure how to act or what to do.

"You look great." Dom grinned, seemingly oblivious to Kira's nerves. He leaned over and gave her a kiss on the cheek. "Are you ready to go?"

Blushing, Kira nodded. Then, grabbing her purse, she locked the door and followed Dom out to his car.

"So, what's the plan?" Kira asked once she'd managed to do up her seatbelt.

"Uh-uh." Dom shook his head as he put the car into

drive. "I'm not telling. You'll just have to wait and find out."

"Really?" Kira laughed. "Fine, don't tell me. But that means you'll have to entertain me for however long the drive takes."

"Well, thank god it's only a few minutes away," Dom quipped with a grin as Kira playfully slapped his arm, all sense of embarrassment and awkwardness gone.

Dom drove like he did everything: expertly and with confidence. His hand rested lightly on the steering wheel, completely in control of the situation. There was no hesitation as he worked onto the street and wove through traffic. He chatted absently as he drove, entertaining Kira. Telling her stories about a former chef who refused to work with students, claiming they were unfettered and too volatile for his inventive personality. Kira was bubbling with laughter at the impression Dom did of the unbalanced man.

After about ten minutes in the car, they pulled up outside the Chatelane Rec Center.

"So, are we going to bingo then?" Kira asked, unable to think of any other activity that took place in the building outside of hockey season.

"No, smart ass, we are not going to bingo." Dom got out of the car and came around to help Kira out.

"So if bingo isn't an option—which, by the way, I am slightly disappointed about—what are we doing here?" Kira looped her arm through his as they walked towards the main set of doors.

"Well, I wanted to do something different. I heard about this game from one of the players who came into the restaurant the other day, and thought it sounded like fun."

"Now I'm real curious. You understand I'm not very athletic or sporty, right?" Kira asked.

"You don't have to be—we're here to watch, we're part of the cheering section." Dom reached out and pulled open the door, allowing an excess amount of noise to escape. The combination of music and loud voices created a cacophony of undistinguishable sounds that surrounded them as they entered the building. There were colourful, hand-painted signs all around proclaiming that the rematch of "The Dangerous Dollz" versus "Virtuosity" was happening tonight.

Dom paid their admittance fee and led the way through the entry area and into the arena. They climbed into the stands, looking around. Dom leaned close and spoke loud enough that Kira could hear him over the noise.

"Did you know that roller derby had made a comeback in Chatelane?"

Kira's eyes were wide as she shook her head. There was so much to take in, and she looked around, trying to absorb the energy.

They found their spots and Kira sat down as Dom indicated he'd be right back; he was going to get drinks and some food. Kira appreciated the moment to check out the event.

From her viewpoint she could see a large, imperfect oval taped off on the concrete floor of the arena that was obviously the track. The oval spanned sixty feet long by twenty-five feet wide. There were striped referees whirling around on eight wheels, loosening up while they chatted with one another over the music that echoed through the large space. The arena was half full and the crowd was already getting revved up, carrying signs that cheered for one team or the other.

She skimmed over the flier they had been handed as they entered, which explained some of the plays and what to expect. Kira vaguely remembered roller derby from when she was a kid and had seen it on television. Then a few years ago the movie *Whip It* with Drew Barrymore had reintroduced her to the sport. Apparently it had resurfaced across the country after that. Tonight's match was full contact and, according to the pamphlet, it could get quite violent. The players came from a wide range of backgrounds: there was a lawyer, a nurse, a banker, and a small-business owner on the teams, to name a few careers. It seemed like derby ran the gamut when it came to those who played.

The flier also showed some of tonight's players, along with pictures. The Dangerous Dollz were in black and pink T-shirts. Their team members ranged from the rather evil-looking "Bad Ass Boopster" to "Bashing Becky" to "Diva Diana," who looked a little like a doll herself. Virtuosity was the team in blue and green. "Evil Elise" was the team captain and jammer; her bio stated that she was twenty-five and had found derby after a disturbingly violent bout with the law. Kira didn't think the bios were the truth, but she couldn't be sure as she stared at the picture of a blue-haired young woman with tattoos, who scowled at the camera.

She looked up just in time to see Dom as he wove his way through the stands towards her, his blue eyes intent on watching where he was going, his powerful body rippling as he stepped over the seats to the row where Kira sat.

"My god, Dom." Kira gasped and reached out to help him. "I would have helped had I known you planned to buy everything." Somehow, in his hands Dom had two loaded hotdogs, two plastic cups filled with what looked like beer and two bags of chips.

"I'm in the hospitality industry. The day that I can't carry the food I purchase is the day for me to retire." Dom laughed and plopped down beside her.

The smell of hot dogs and fresh buns surrounded Kira and she took her meal gratefully. Dom had gotten her foot-long fully loaded, with fried onions and all the condiments, just the way Kira liked it. With a smile of bliss she bit into the meal, sipping beer in between bites.

They had barely managed to finish eating when the music swelled, the announcer took his place, and the teams rolled into the arena to thunderous applause. The women all wore their team shirts and protective gear, but the rest of their outfits varied as much as they did. There were fishnet stockings, boy shorts, tutus, and everything else imaginable.

The next hour and a quarter was an education. The announcer explained what was happening as the players whipped around the track, tackling each other and colliding with bone-crunching force, which they ignored to race off as fast as possible. There were bloody noses and injuries galore, but these women fought like true athletes—they never gave in or gave up.

Kira found herself laughing, flinching, and groaning along with the rest of the crowd, as well as yelling at plays and generally getting very excited by the game in a way she never would have expected. Beside her Dom also cheered and yelled with honest animation.

The game was a nail-biter, but The Dollz won the match by a point in sudden-death overtime. Afterwards Dom and Kira allowed the exuberant crowd to sweep them out the doors into the evening chill, where they grinned at each other and made their way towards the car.

"That was awesome," Kira enthused. "I would never have thought to come to an event like this."

"I'm glad you enjoyed yourself." Dom laughed, and as they walked he slipped his hand in hers. It felt natural, like an extension of their friendship, and made Kira feel comfortable.

"So where to next?" she asked.

"Again, so impatient to know everything. You must learn patience, young Padawan."

"You seriously did not just reference *Star Wars* to me, did you?" Kira laughed.

Dom grinned and squeezed her hand. "I am even more impressed with you now that I know you got the reference."

"Whatever," Kira scoffed. "So I guess, once again, I have to wait?"

Dom just nodded and opened the passenger door for her.

9 CHAPTER NINE

"I can't possibly eat another bite." Kira moaned and sat back, her hand on her belly.

"I know how you feel." Dom sighed from across the table. "But it was so good."

They both stared mournfully at the almost empty plate in front of them. After the roller derby match, Dom had taken them to Let Them Eat Cake, a new incredibly sinful bakery and coffee house. It was in an older area of Chatelane, in a long, narrow building that had once upon a time been an alley no bigger than ten feet wide. The exterior was faded yellow brick, edges blackened by weather and time. Once inside Kira had been pleasantly surprised by the bright atmosphere. The walls were painted a bright green and all the tables were laminated in a fire-engine red that caught the eye and felt vaguely bohemian. It was one of those places where you could suspend a coffee for those that didn't have enough money to buy one, a community where people sat for hours, surrounded by the vague smell of patchouli and creativity.

The café was filled with artistic types: several young people typing furiously away on their laptops, as well as a young woman writing in her journal as though her life depended on it. A table near the back had a ukulele-playing dreadlocked fellow, who was humming as he strummed a soft tune that Kira didn't recognize. The buzz of quiet conversation and the whirring of the antiquated cappuccino machines filled the corners and crevasses of the room. They'd been at their table for the last hour and a half, having finished a coffee each before ordering and enjoying dessert. They had talked and laughed and shared stories from their lives. Kira felt closer to Dom than ever before; it was amazing to her what a difference a few hours of conversation could make.

Eventually the chocolate lovers' triple layer caramel mousse cake had called to both of them and they had shared the decadent dessert blissfully.

It was nearing ten o'clock, and Kira wasn't sure if this was the end of their date. She cleared her throat and spoke. "So. My dear Mr. De Luca, do you have more evil schemes for the evening, or have we exhausted your limited plans?"

"Nice try Kira. You don't get off so easy. I figured I'd be nice and let you decide how we'll finish up our date. You have two options." He arched his eyebrow at her while a soft smile played around the edges of his lips.

"Sweet!" Kira sounded vaguely like the teenager she must have once been. "Does that mean you're going to tell me your plans now, instead of making me wait?"

"Not exactly." The slight smile blossomed into a full grin. "I like keeping you in suspense. It makes my night more fun."

"Damn." Kira muttered with mock frustration. "Fine—so what are my choices? And don't tell me one of them involves a bottle of baby oil and naked Twister, cuz I told you I don't do that. Well, not on the first date at least."

Dom choked on his tongue for a minute before he managed to clear his throat and speak again. "That sounds… interesting. I never would have pegged you for the naked board games type of girl."

"Well then." Kira leaned her chin on the palm of her hand and her eyes twinkled. "You don't know me as well as you thought."

"Trust me, *bellissima*; I hope to get to know you a lot better." His voice was husky as he reached out and touched her cheek lightly.

After a few moments of staring into each other's eyes

while lust filled the air between them, they simultaneously leaned away. Dom sat back in his chair, his blue eyes darker than normal as he took a deep breath.

Kira felt her heart pounding and she felt light-headed as though she had held her breath for too long. She inhaled sharply, allowing the oxygen to return to her starved brain; finally managing to speak again, she kept her voice light as she asked, "So what are my choices then?"

"You get to choose between loud, fun, and boisterous or quiet, childlike, and intimate."

"Hmm, intriguing. I don't suppose you'll give me any more hints?" She looked at Dom hopefully.

"Nope." He grinned. "That's all you get, so make your choice."

"Okay." Kira thought for a few seconds, tapping her finger against her chin. "Well, we've done loud and boisterous plenty of times. We know we can have fun loudly." She smiled inwardly, remembering the drunken nights at Dominic's that definitely counted as thunderous. Let alone last night; while she didn't remember, it seemed to have been spirited at the least. "So let's go with the unexpected, childlike, and quiet."

"Don't forget intimate." Dom stood and held out his hand. "Good choice. If you're ready, then we'll get going."

A few minutes later Kira wondered where the evening was taking them. They walked into the inky night, away from the coffee house. The streetlights cast shadows, almost making it appear sinister. Almost. Chatelane was a small town; there was nothing to be scared about when walking around after dark.

They held hands, and Dom easily led the way as they ventured a few blocks off the main drag. Eventually Dom turned them into a small grassy area.

They walked down a trail between two houses, its entrance obscured by the shadows cast by a large hedge, which only served to make the entrance feel forbidden. Just past the fenced-in backyards, the path opened up into a playground. It was completely invisible from the street, which left the area feeling private and magical. The crescent moon allowed a filtered light to shine down anywhere not easily brightened by the soft yellow light filtering the space from the street lamps.

"Is this the place?" Kira whispered, feeling like a loud voice was out of place here.

"Yes." Dom smiled. "I thought it would be fun to relive our childhoods. Play and let loose."

"Sounds great." Kira led the way to the wooden play structure and began climbing to the top level, with Dom following close behind. Once at the top, they took turns slithering down the plastic slide, their laughter echoing lightly in the night.

They played on the seesaw, swung on monkey bars, sat at the top of the castle-shaped play house talking, and contorted themselves to ride the spring rocker rides shaped like animals. They shared their lives, talking and enjoying each other's company the whole time.

After an hour of entertaining themselves around the park, Dom walked over to the set of swings and sat down on one while Kira sank into the other. It had been years since she'd played in a park, and she'd loved every minute of their time here.

She pushed off and began to pump her legs, letting the breeze push her hair back as she flew higher and higher. As though it was a contest, beside her Dom also pushed off. In time with one another, they swung higher, grins of delight on both their faces.

Once she'd reached the summit, her fingers gripped the chain and she leaned back, welcoming the dizzy feeling that twisted through her stomach. She stared up at the night sky as it whizzed back and forth, the stars blurring slightly.

Eventually she slowed, still barely holding on by her fingertips, allowing her feet to drag her to a gentle stop. Eyes bright with excitement, she pulled herself upright and was somewhat shocked to discover Dom standing right in front of her.

"You are so beautiful," he whispered, his hand on the chain stilling her movement. *"Tesoro mio."*

"What does that mean?" Kira asked breathlessly.

Dom leaned down, his lips millimeters from hers, his words skimming across her skin. "My treasure," he answered. Then, speaking so softly Kira could barely hear him, he whispered, "The best part of my day is the moment you walk through my door. Up until then it's like everything is in black and white. I am in a waiting period. Waiting for you. Then you walk in and it's as if the world is now filled with colour and I can breathe again."

Unable to resist, Kira leaned in and placed her lips against Dom's. She had fought the attraction she felt for so long that she couldn't, didn't want to fight it any longer.

When their lips touched, Dom groaned and stepped closer. Kira felt the hairs on her arms stand up and, without thinking, she looped her hands around his neck, her fingers tangling in his silky black hair.

They kissed, their lips fusing together and moving in sync with one another. At first it was tentative, a getting to know one another in soft, sweeping, gentle kisses, which quickly turned more frantic as their desire burnt hotter. With his hands migrating to capture either side of her face, he teased his tongue against her lips until she opened her mouth and handed him control and gave him total possession of her. The expertise he showed as he moved her beyond thinking into a realm of only feeling threw Kira into a spin of lust and desire.

Kira lost herself in the passion, warmth travelling from her lips and spreading through her to puddle in a pool of volcanic lava below her waist. She ached to touch Dom and for him to touch her, to feel his fingers moving against her bare skin.

With a final moment of clarity, Kira pulled away, her breath hitching as she tried to breathe with lungs now too small to hold air. "We have to stop. I can't... we're in a playground," she moaned regretfully.

Dom leaned away, also breathing hard. After a few minutes he turned his eyes back to Kira.

"Well. That was… something else," he muttered, his eyes sparkling in the night.

"That it was." A smile twitched on her face before she frowned and continued. "I'm sorry; I didn't mean to lose control like that."

"It wasn't just you," Dom interrupted.

"I know, but I should have better restraint. I usually do—I don't know what came over me." Kira looked down, overcome by self-doubt and shame at her overpowering response to Dom.

"Hey." His fingers cupped her chin, pulling her eyes up to meet his. "Enough of that. We were both caught up in the moment, me as much as you. There is no doubt in my mind that together we would be amazing, I am so attracted to you that I can't control myself. It makes me happy that I'm not the only one."

"I'm not used to a guy wanting me as much as I want them. My ex-husband…." Kira groaned, closing her eyes for a long moment. "Again, I apologize. I'm breaking just about every rule when it comes to first dates here." At Dom's look of confusion, she elaborated. "According to *Teen Beat*— which, by the way, is not something I normally read but I happened upon it the other day. I most certainly don't subscribe to it. That would be weird—for an almost forty-year-old woman to regularly read a magazine aimed at teenagers. Just weird." Kira looked at the ground as she babbled away until she pulled herself together and locked her gaze back on Dom's beautiful eyes. "Anyways, I digress. What I was saying is that apparently you should never talk about previous relationships on first dates, let alone show how desperately attracted to the other party you are. I am a total failure at dating."

"Desperately attracted to?" Dom's eyebrow shot up. "I like the sound of that. You are so good for my ego." He laughed.

"Oh, shut up." Kira giggled and pulled away. "If your head gets any bigger, you'll float away."

"I'll try to keep my self-admiration under control, if you stop being so hard on yourself." He looked at Kira sternly until she nodded. "All right then, we should call it a night, before I get all macho like some chest-beating Neanderthal and drag you home with me." He stopped with his fists poised over his pectorals and looked hopefully at Kira until she shook her head solemnly. "Well, you can't blame a guy for dreaming." He laughed and grabbed Kira's hand to help her off the swing with an infectious grin. "Let's get out of here."

10 CHAPTER TEN

With a groan of frustration Kira ignored the flashing light on her cell phone. All morning the damn thing had been going off, with texts coming in constantly from both Michael and Dom until she thought she would scream. She couldn't think straight; she had even put it on vibrate, hoping for a reprieve. Unfortunately it still buzzed loud enough that she knew it was receiving another text.

After her date with Dom last night, Kira had gotten up and treated herself to an unhealthy but gratifying breakfast of Oreo cookies and Diet Coke. Her intention to spend the day deliberating her situation with the men in her life had gone wildly astray.

More than time to think, she needed someone to talk to. She needed a friend she could confide in and hash over what her choice should be. Unfortunately, in the last few years that person had always been Dom, and now, well, that was out of the question.

She had gone back and forth between them, mentally listing their qualities and flaws, trying to see the path she should take, to no avail. Hell, she'd even resorted to teenage decision-making methods: making a chart that had their names at the top and listing the pros and cons for each of them. The buzzing phone interrupted her thoughts and only served to remind her that she was no closer to a decision than she had been when she first got up.

She made an inarticulate sound of pure frustration deep in her throat and grabbed the phone. Without reading any of the messages she quickly typed: "Gone for day, need to think. Will ttyl." She addressed the message to both Dom and Michael and, before she could reconsider, hit send.

That done, she decided to make her excuse reality and, turning the phone off, she threw it into her purse and stalked out the door, locking it behind her.

A half hour later she was cruising down the highway, Pink blaring through the speakers as the wind blew her bright red hair into a frenzied mess. When she had first gotten into the car she hadn't known where she was going, but after a few minutes of driving aimlessly she had finally picked her direction.

Without even thinking about how to get there, she turned off the highway and easily buzzed up the secondary road. Soon enough the large sign directed her to Lakeside Provincial Park. She pulled into the small parking lot, finding a spot for her car with ease. Not wanting to worry about losing her purse, she grabbed her keys, confirmed the cash in her pocket, and tossed her leather bag under the seat before jumping out of the car.

It had been twenty years since she'd been here; the last time was before her parents had died. She had always wanted to come back, but Steve was too busy, and he had no interest in hiking, or camping for that matter. In a way now she was grateful for that; after all it meant all her memories here were good ones. Although at the time it had infuriated her.

There were trails for hiking, everything from a half hour to a whole-day-long adventure. Lakeside had a specified campground and of course a lake to swim in. Over all it was a great summer retreat. She'd spent so many of her carefree summers here, surrounded by family and fun.

As she walked in she immediately noticed some changes. At the registration office a new wing jutted out the left side, proudly housing a small motel with maybe fifteen rooms and a diner that looked like a typical greasy spoon. The previously gravelled road had now been paved and the camp ground had been enlarged to allow for seasonal trailers. She also thought she saw an outdoor pool.

She walked into the log-style registration building and rang the bell. While she waited, she looked over the pricing sheet attached to the wall behind the counter. It was surprisingly reasonable at this time of year. A young man, about eighteen, with a well-developed tan came in from a door at the back.

"Hi!" He beamed, his teeth looking unbelievably white against his bronze skin. "How can I help you?"

Kira stepped closer to the counter and answered. "I'm looking to come in for the afternoon."

"Sounds great." He pulled a sheet out from under the counter and handed it to Kira. "Just fill this out—don't forget to put your licence plate number here." He indicated a line with the point of a pen that he then passed to Kira.

Once she was done she handed the form back. "Perfect," the cashier said after glancing down for a moment. "It's five bucks to come in for the day." As Kira dug in her pocket for the cash, he continued talking. "You sure picked a great day to come out. Not many people in, so very little to disturb you. Being it's a Sunday, all the weekend campers have already left and the weather's still nice. I'm here until eight tonight if you need anything."

"Thanks." Kira handed him the money and quickly left the small building.

She beelined for the lake; as a child it had been her favourite place to be. A lot of teenaged angst had been sorted on the very dock that she now meandered out on. She smiled slightly as she sat at the end of the wooden dock, the gentle waves causing the entire structure to sway softly.

She crossed her legs and stared into the water, allowing it to soften her thoughts, to smooth her mind. Once in a meditative state she let her thoughts follow the needed pathways.

Michael was exciting, and so creative. He was young and so beautiful she could spend days just looking at him. In the bedroom he focused on her with an intensity that could be scary, always making sure she had orgasmed at least twice before taking his own pleasure. He was the first man to show any interest in her since Steve had left her, and he made her feel great about herself. Yes, he had screwed up majorly with the sculpture of her, but she was sure they could work that out. She thought *what couple didn't have disagreements and even outright arguments?*

Dom was more electrifying than she'd expected. He was fun; they laughed together and had many common interests. He was her friend, the one who had listened and comforted and cared for her when no one else did. He was also so seriously hot that she couldn't believe he was attracted to her. He was more age appropriate and sent shivers of pure lust through her with a slight touch. She couldn't compare bedroom skills, but if kissing was any indication, that wouldn't be an issue.

Back and forth she went, listing their qualities and flaws until even in her meditative state she was getting flustered. Eventually she shook her head and stood up, deciding to walk one of the shorter trails.

Kira wandered to the start of the path and set off, determined to make a decision or die trying. She set off at a leisurely pace, allowing the soft afternoon light to invigorate her.

At least five hours later Kira was beginning to worry; her phone and watch had been left in the car, so she had no real idea of how much time had passed.

Her jaunt down a leisurely trail had gone horribly wrong. She now knew her starting point must have been flawed—what she took as a 'beginner' trail must have been one of the more advanced ones.

At first she had ambled along, lost in thought, the beautiful scenery helping her to relax in her thoughts. For quite some time she hadn't even realized she was on the wrong path. It was only when she began to get thirsty and tired that she had thought about how long she had been wandering through the woods. And now it felt like it had been forever since she'd seen any sign of civilization or other people. The sounds of nature around her began to get frightening as the shadows lengthened through the forest, making what had been magical only hours ago now a scene straight from a horror movie.

"Damn," she muttered, fighting the tears she knew wouldn't help the situation. The sun was rapidly falling behind the trees, and her feet were aching so bad that Kira looked down. With dismay she saw the blood running from her ankle where the strap had rubbed her skin raw. These sandals were fine for a nice day out, but definitely not what she should be wearing for a serious hike. She had noticed the blisters a while ago, but had continued on with no other option. Eventually her feet had gone numb and she hadn't even felt the blood that trickled down each foot from several jagged cuts. She looked up to see the trail in front of her continued, seemingly endless.

At least she had had lots of time to consider and debate and decide. With a groan, she continued plodding along, putting one foot in front of the other and ignoring the thirst that was in the back of her throat. Absentmindedly, she wondered what would happen if she didn't finish the trail soon. Would she curl up in a ball on the trail to sleep? Would a bear come out and eat her, or even just a skunk to spray her? She started to panic, walking as fast as her aching legs and bleeding feet would allow.

Just as she was about to start running, she burst out of the forest about thirty feet from where she had started out.

"Thank God." Kira managed to restrain herself from kissing the ground in pure joy. Barely. She stumbled up to the registration building.

11 CHAPTER ELEVEN

After being thoroughly checked over by the staff of the park, Kira managed to finally extricate herself from their well-intentioned but interfering clutches. Her feet had been bandaged and she'd had her fill of water after discovering that she had been in the forest for over six hours.

The staff had been about to launch a search effort after discovering her car was still in the parking lot after the day park closed. It was eight thirty, and Kira breathed a sigh of relief as she got back into her car.

While waiting for the air conditioning to take effect, she flipped her phone on and scrolled through the messages. There were fifteen apologetic pleas from Michael, followed by eight concerned messages, the most recent an hour ago. From Dom there were five inquiring messages from this morning and five concerned ones that started around six that evening.

She leaned her forehead against the window and read the first message from Michael.

> *Kira, I am so sorry. Please call me.*

Followed by:

> *I was wrong. Please forgive me, we can work it out. You are the*
> *Best thing to ever happen to me. Call me.*

And so the messages went on. All the ones prior to her "stop texting me" message were in that vein. After she had asked for some time to think the messages had stopped, for a few hours at least. Then they had started again, around five o'clock.

> *I haven't heard from you. Is everything okay? How* can I make it
> *up to you? Call me.*

Followed by:

> *I am getting worried, are you okay? Please Kira, just* text me back
> *so I know you are alright.*

Dom's messages started out more conversational. Thanking her for last night and wondering if she'd had a chance to think things over. They were calmer in nature to start with. They did get a little worried later in the day when she still hadn't texted back.

Glad that she hadn't hurt her fingers during her adventure, Kira opened the screen to send a new message. She addressed it to Michael and quickly typed:

> *9:07 P.M*
> *I'm okay. It's been a crazy day. Will talk to you tomorrow.*

Then she hit send. She knew that she didn't want to have a long conversation with Michael via texting; she'd rather have it in person. But she also didn't want him to worry unnecessarily, so the message would hopefully prevent that until she could see him.

With Dom, she wanted to talk to him in person. It was Sunday night, Dominic's was closed at nine, but she knew Dom usually spent until midnight going over the numbers from the previous week; he would still be at the restaurant.

She flipped the car into drive and sped out of the lot. She drove along the deserted highway, going over and over what she wanted to say, mentally preparing herself. In the twenty minutes it took her to arrive back in Chatelane she had thought of six totally different approaches, and as she pulled up in front of Dominic's she still didn't know what the best plan of action was.

The restaurant looked abandoned—the lit sign announcing Dominic's was dark and the parking lot empty of all but Dom's car. Getting out of her car, Kira approached the entry door, hoping Dom would hear her. Through the window in the faint light of the bar she could see Dom moving around. His tall frame was shadowed as he sat at the bar with a drink in hand; looking at what Kira assumed was paperwork.

She knocked softly on the door, watching as his head turned towards her. She waved slightly and Dom walked across the entry and flipped the deadbolt, allowing her inside.

"Kira." His warm, accented voice surrounded her as he waved her through the door. In typically European fashion his warm hands gripped her upper arms and he drew her to him. His soft lips kissed each of her cheeks before he said, "I wasn't expecting you. Come in."

"I was in the neighbourhood," Kira said lightly.

"Well, I'm glad you're here." Dom smiled as he led Kira across the restaurant to the bar. "Drink?" he asked.

"Sure. I'd love a margarita, if it's not too much trouble." Kira pulled up a stool and watched as he moved behind the bar with the ease born of years of practice. He smiled and expertly mixed her drink as Kira told him all about her misadventure at the provincial park.

"You could have been hurt." His eyes were concerned. "Are you sure you are all right?"

Kira waved a hand. "I'm fine. My pride is bruised a little, and the cuts on my feet will take a bit to heal, but I am alright."

Dom came around the bar, handing Kira her drink as he

took a sip of the beer he held, his piercing blue eyes never leaving hers.

"I will believe you." He smiled, causing butterflies to let loose inside Kira. "But can I check your bandages, to see with my own eyes that there is no lasting harm?"

As he spoke he set his beer on the bar and dropped to his knees in front of her. His strong hand took hold of her ankle, raising her foot for his inspection.

He gently removed her sandals and ran his fingers over the bandages as he looked her over.

"Dom." Kira's voice hitched in her throat as his fingertips slid across her bare skin, leaving a trail of electricity in their wake. She managed to swallow and continued. "You don't have to... I am fine."

She tried to pull her foot out of his hands, embarrassed by what they might smell like after a day of hiking. He only tightened his grip and looked up at her, eyes hooded, a smile tickling the corners of his sumptuous lips. "I will feel better if you allow me to confirm your diagnosis."

She stopped pulling away as his hands skittered to her calves, lightly massaging as he went. Kira's eyes closed with bliss and a light moan escaped her lips. She finally managed to pull together the ability to talk as his hands skimmed over her kneecaps, lightly touching her thighs. "Dom, we can't. I came to talk to you."

"Why can't we? I don't want to talk right now." From where he knelt, looking up at her, he asked, "I want you. Do you want me?"

"Yes, but—" Kira started, only to be interrupted by Dom.

"No buts. We are adults; I've wanted you for so long. You want me." His hands continued to trace light patterns all over her bare legs, occasionally dipping under the hem of her shorts as he spoke, making it nearly impossible for Kira to think rationally. "I'm tired of being good. We know we fit together, please let me love you," he ended, barely whispering as her head fell back in bliss.

She tried once more, raising her head and answering with a whisper. "I want to, but I am not that girl." She tried to pull away and Dom came to his feet in front of her, planting himself between her thighs. She could feel the warmth emanating from his body.

His passion-darkened eyes pierced her as he spoke. "If you can honestly say you do not want me as much as I want you, fine. We stop. We talk. I had just hoped for a moment of fantasy before we face reality." As he spoke, Kira's eyes trailed to his luscious lips and, unable to understand the English language any longer, she threw herself at him.

Locking her lips to his, she allowed the overwhelming lust she felt to explode from inside. Her fingers twined through his hair, tugging him to an angle that eased the pressure building within her. Dom was immediately right with her, his hands on her waist; his body pressed intimately against her and his tongue plunged inside her mouth. Kira moaned as she felt his erection as clearly as she felt his lips plucking at hers.

Her legs locked around his waist as she gave in. Forgetting discretion and propriety, Kira allowed herself to be ruled by feelings. Together they fused their bodies as tightly as possible, their tongues twisting in a dance as old as time.

She pulled away, gasping for breath as he kissed a path down her neck, tongue flicking out on her jugular vein.

"My God." Her head fell back, granting Dom better access; in between kisses he breathed against her skin.

"You. Are amazing. You taste like heaven. *Bellissima.*" His voice was roughened by passion, and his hands slid behind her, cupping her buttocks, pulling her tighter against him.

With seeming effortless grace he lifted her, crushing her to his hardened body. Her pelvis rocked against his erection, causing both of them to moan. She tightened her legs around his waist and using both hands she anchored his face allowing her to ravish his lips as he moved her towards the nearest table.

She couldn't think, as lust overwhelmed her. A pure, uncontrollable need she had never felt before took over her mind and body. His lips made her lose all thought, all ability to reason.

Dom set her on the edge of the table and pulled away for a few moments, his hand sweeping the table off behind her. A crash of plates and glasses hitting the floor startled Kira into a giggle.

"Well, you certainly... shatter my world." She grinned at Dom. Her eyes twinkled with glee and yet were still filled with lust.

"Definitely... breaking... all the rules." Dom returned her grin before fusing his lips against hers once more. Instantly they were transported back into the moment, eagerness controlling their every move.

They tore at their clothes in between soul-scorching kisses, touching each other's body quickly. Each movement exposed more of their skin, areas that needed to be touched, to be licked, to be praised. Bare moments later they were naked enough to press against each other; the feel of his firm body leaning into her soft curves ripped a deep groan from both of them.

She clutched at his well-defined arms while his lips ravaged the junction between her neck and shoulder. Frantically she grabbed at him, muttering, "Please, Dom!"

He pulled away long enough to look at her with greedy, hungry eyes, his body poised over her as she reclined on the table. He positioned himself and fed himself into her, inch by maddening inch until they both sighed with the rightness of it. She felt filled to the limit as he pushed the last little bit, pressing his pelvis firmly against hers.

Dom leaned his forehead against hers for a few seconds, savouring the moment. Then, staring into her eyes, he began to move inside her—slowly at first, but gradually building up speed and intensity, his lips once more sliding across hers.

He groaned, "*Solo tu*," as his hands alternated between her breasts, which were thrusting themselves at him like the true hussies they were, and her thighs as they surrounded his waist.

Kira held onto his shoulders with one hand as she felt the pressure within her build to a peak, his thrusts pressing his pubic bone against her overly sensitized clit. Her other hand leaned back against the table, anchoring herself as she met him thrust for thrust, forcing the connection against her happy spot as he filled her. She pounded against him, biting her lip as she rocketed towards her climax, their sweat-slicked bodies moving together perfectly, hurtling them both towards ecstasy. The muscles inside her pulled him tighter, milking him as she threw her head back and came with a scream.

Dom grabbed her hips; he changed the angle slightly and thrust twice more, then roared unabashedly as he found his release. They stayed locked together for a few moments while they each caught their breath, fingers gently stroking each other, coming down from the high that was their lovemaking.

Eventually Dom kissed her lips and pulled away looking around ruefully at the mess on the floor from the broken plates. "Don't move. I'll get a broom to clean up. I don't want you to cut yourself."

Kira nodded, grabbing her T-shirt from where it had been dropped behind her and tugging it on quickly to partially cover the amount of bare skin she was showing. Dom, unashamed of his own nakedness, came back with a broom that he promptly used to sweep up the broken glass. Kira watched him from beneath lowered lashes; he most certainly had nothing to be ashamed of. His body was the stuff songs were made of: olive skinned, with defined muscles and no visible tan lines. His stomach had a distinct line down the center of it and a hint of a six pack; his entire torso was hairless and sculpted like a piece of art. She allowed her eyes to drop below the waist and her eyebrows flew almost into her hair. Dom was hung. She swallowed the excess moisture pooling in her mouth, glad she hadn't seen his penis before it was inside her, or she never would have thought it would fit. Even at rest it was more than Kira had thought possible on a man outside of a porn movie.

Once done with the broom, Dom looked up at her, a flicker of disappointment crossing his face as he took in the semi-clothed state. He shrugged easily and, grabbing the jeans he had been wearing, he slipped them on. They hung low on his hips, and without a top his man V was showcased to absolute perfection.

He moved over beside her, his fingers trailing lightly down her arm. "That was amazing."

Kira nodded with a soft smile on her lips but didn't speak.

"But we seem to have gotten carried away and forgotten something," Dom continued.

Kira's brow furrowed. "What did we forget?"

Dom blushed slightly as he answered. "A condom. I am sorry. I've never been so out of control that I didn't remember that."

"It was both of us," Kira murmured, distraught at her own complete forgetfulness. "But its okay, I went on the pill a few weeks ago. I'm clean otherwise."

"As am I." Dom stared at Kira, his heart on his sleeve. She looked away, suddenly embarrassed by their act of pleasure. "I'm feeling rather exposed here. I'm gonna get dressed."

Dom frowned, but backed up so she could slide off the table. She grabbed her shorts and her bra from where they had landed and beelined for the ladies' room.

Once somewhat in a state of dress (she had been unable to find her panties), she looked into the mirror. "You can do this," she whispered in solidarity to her reflection. Running her fingers through her hair to smooth it down, she stepped back into the dining room.

Dom still only wore his blue jeans as he sat at the bar sipping on his beer. He looked up, a questioning smile on his lips as she came close. She smiled back shyly, then grabbed her margarita and took a deep drink.

Turning towards Dom, she spoke. "I actually came here to talk."

"What, you mean you did not come to get lucky?" he quipped.

"Nope. Getting banged on the table wasn't on the plan for tonight."

"Well, let me be the first to say I am all for the change in plans." Dom laughed.

Kira grinned back at him. "It was, wow. Amazing." She licked her lips just thinking about the raw passion that had run between them, then shook her head, dislodging the devilish thoughts. "But as I said, I came here to talk."

"Okay. I'm listening." Dom leaned back on his stool, showcasing his fine physique to its best advantage.

Kira fell silent for a long time, organizing her thoughts before she began. "I spent the day trying to figure out what to do." Kira looked down into her glass as though the blue concoction held answers. Eventually she continued. "I am in a real tough spot here. I like you, you are my best friend, and obviously we have some serious chemistry." She waved a hand at the table they had just had extremely satisfying sex on top of.

"I'm sensing a 'but' here," Dom said quietly, to which Kira nodded.

"But I owe Michael something. Even if it is just a chance to plead his case, I need to give him and the relationship I have with him a chance." Kira fell silent, unable to look at Dom. "I am sorry. If I were free I would be happy to date you. I'm not, and I am not the girl that runs around on her boyfriend. I need to give him a chance."

"*Cazzo!*" Kira didn't need a translation for the angry word. "So what, this was a pity fuck?" Dom snapped, his accent becoming more pronounced.

"No!" Kira snapped. "It was...." She paused. "I don't know! I shouldn't have. Damn it, I am sorry," she stuttered.

Dom took a deep breath and ran his fingers through his

hair in an obvious attempt for control before he spoke. "What we have is special, Kira. Don't throw that away on some antiquated view of what is right. You don't owe Michael the rest of your life just because you are dating him now."

"I don't want us not to be friends." Kira moaned, ignoring everything he'd said.

"Don't walk away from us." Dom stopped and shook his head. "I'm not going to beg you. I don't beg anyone. The decision is, and always has been, yours to make. But I can't be your fall-back guy—whenever Michael pisses you off you come running to me. I won't be that guy."

"Does that mean you won't be my friend?" Kira whispered, ashamed, as tears filled her eyes.

"I don't know." Dom set his beer on the bar. "Perhaps you need to think some more. Obviously you have feelings for me, or else that"—he nodded towards the table— "wouldn't have happened."

"I came here with my mind set. I knew what I had to do. I knew what the right thing to do was." Kira felt confusion overwhelm her, clouding her mind so that all she could do was stick to what she had decided.

"So you are saying that you choose Michael," Dom clarified.

"I am saying there is no choice," Kira whispered. Dom stood and walked out of the room.

"I choose myself." Kira wiped the tear that fell silently onto her cheek and then stood, with her back straight and her head high, as she walked out of the restaurant.

12 CHAPTER TWELVE

With great trepidation, Kira took the freight elevator up to Michael's apartment. Her heart was hammering in her chest as she prepared to see what was left, if anything, of her relationship with Michael. And also to see if what was there was anything Kira was interested in maintaining any longer.

The elevator shuddered to a stop and, using her strength, Kira pulled up the security gate and stepped over the threshold gingerly.

From across the room Michael smiled and moved towards her. "Kira," he said. "How are you?"

"I'm alright. You?" Kira played nervously with the zipper of her purse, unsure why she felt so uncomfortable.

"I'm okay—tired though. I didn't sleep much. I've been going over our fight again and again, and I think we need to talk."

"I agree. We need to talk." Kira moved into the room and sank onto the couch gratefully.

"First, I need to apologize." Michael sat across from Kira, his brown eyes staring earnestly into hers. "I was wrong. I should never have made that sculpture without your permission. I was blinded by your beauty and my own perceived brilliance. It was wrong. I have already started to make changes to the sculpture so she will not be you."

"Thank you," Kira murmured, grateful that she no longer had to worry about a nude sculpture of herself being displayed all over town.

Michael nodded, pleased with himself. "So are we okay?" he asked.

Kira looked at him, thoughts tumbling through her mind. This was her chance. All she had to do was say "Yes." And everything would be back to the way they were before. This had been her decision yesterday, to go to Michael and throw herself into the relationship with him, make it work. It was a chance for a do-over. He was a beautiful young man who wanted nothing more than to make her happy. He had changed his life's work just to please her. In the bedroom he excited her in ways she never would have thought possible back when she was with her ex-husband.

So what was she waiting for? She gave a crooked smile, the words on the edge of her tongue. Then she shook her head and spoke, her voice choked with emotion. "I'm sorry Michael, but we aren't okay."

"What else can I do to make you forgive me?" He leaned towards her, his hands outstretched.

"I have already forgiven you." Kira shook her head, indicating that wasn't the problem. "It turns out I'm not a very good person."

"What are you talking about? You are a great person." Michael's eyes and voice betrayed his confusion.

"I'm really not." Kira paused, working up the courage she knew she needed. "I slept with someone else last night." Kira looked into his eyes, unwilling to hide from the consequences of her actions. "I shouldn't have, but I did. I'm sorry, but it happened and I refuse to lie to you about it."

Michael held up his hand, indicating he needed silence, and stalked off. His footsteps were loud and sharp as he angrily paced the studio. He stalked back and forth for quite some time like a caged lion, never looking at Kira.

Finally he grabbed a beer from the fridge, snapped it open, and chugged the whole thing in one fell swoop. Then he sat back down, where he looked at the floor for a few minutes before raising his pain-filled eyes to hers. "I won't deny that hurts. It hurts a lot." Michael took a deep breath before continuing. "And yet I can't be terribly angry. We didn't promise that we were exclusive; we had had a huge fight. I get it. I don't like it, but I do get it. Shit happens, and we can move on from here."

Kira stared at Michael in shock. "You would really forgive me for sleeping with someone else?"

"I would be willing to move on from it. To try. I can't guarantee that I *can* get over it, but I am willing to give it another chance. What we have is worth the fight. We weren't dating exclusively. I can't get angry at you for doing something I've done before when I dated other women. That would be hypocritical. So what else is the problem?"

"I feel so stupid saying this, but it isn't you, it's me. I don't think I am as emotionally invested in this relationship as you seem to be." Kira grasped Michael's hand. "The last couple of days have made me realize that I just don't feel the same way about you. You are a great guy, who is going to find a beautiful young woman to fall in love with. I am not that woman."

"Why?" His eyes beseeched her, trying to understand.

"I have to be true to me. I have to choose me. With you, I am a different person, serious and intense. I need to laugh and be stupid, not worry about who is watching and what they think. You made me feel like a beautiful woman again and I will never forget that, or you, but we aren't meant for one another."

"I don't understand." Michael pulled his hand away. "I thought what we had was good."

"It was. Michael, it *was* good. But it's time for both of us to move on." Kira stood and leaned over, lightly kissing his forehead, a sad smile on her face. "I am here for you as a friend. If you need me, just call."

As she left the apartment, she could feel the weight lifting off her heart. She had chosen herself; Michael would be better for it. Both his art and his personal life would be enriched. It might take him some time, but he would see in the long run that she had made the right decision.

She wasn't about to run into a relationship with anyone right away. Kira knew now that she didn't need a man to make her whole, she needed herself. She may have been single since Steve had left her, but she hadn't been single in her heart. She had hidden behind the miserable divorcee persona until she found someone else to be with. After all, a single thirty-eight-year-old woman was truly a failure in the eyes of many in today's society.

What she really needed was to take a bit of time learning to love the person who was inside her. Not the face she showed the world, but rather the Kira that existed below the mask. Was she the slightly frumpy middle-aged divorcee? Or was she the cougar, chasing men a decade younger than her? Who was Kira?

How long she needed to discover herself she had no idea. It was a process she'd always hidden from before. Now, however, she was ready.

With a smile, Kira got into her car and started it, a metaphor for beginning her life again.

13 CHAPTER THIRTEEN

Kira took a deep breath and walked up the sidewalk, her heels clicking on the concrete. She pulled her coat tighter around her, feeling the chill October air whip against her bare legs. It was Halloween night and Dominic's always had the biggest party in all of Chatelane.

It had been a month since she had last seen Dom. Thirty long days of soul searching, learning who she was and coming to terms with the woman that was Kira. She finally could say, with regularity, that she liked the person that she was.

The best thing she had ever done was take the time to find herself. To love herself the way she deserved to be loved.

Now that she was settled, she wanted to see if Dom could forgive her. She had missed him with an ache that reached inside her right to her toes and pulled. Even if they couldn't be together, she missed her best friend.

Once inside she handed her coat over the counter to the coat check girl and turned to the room. Her costume, which had seemed garish in the light of her apartment, fit in perfectly here.

She wore a skin tight brown outfit, somewhat steampunk in style, with leather pieces crisscrossing the chest and legs. A fake laser pistol was strapped to her thigh and her face was covered by a full head mask. The upside down hexagon over her mouth was meant to look like a breather, and her voice would come out of it slightly distorted.

Beyond it feeling gaudy, Kira had worried that she was

hiding behind the costume that if she saw Dom and chickened out, he never needed to know she had been there. Once she had come to that realization, she vowed to see it through no matter what.

She moved into the room, adroitly avoiding crashing into a witch who had obviously had too much to drink. The lights throbbed and the music overwhelmed the crowded space. She set her goal to reach the bar and began to make the journey. On the way she saw an unbelievable gargoyle doing shots, a brightly coloured fairy chatting with Superman, and Fiona and Shrek slow dancing. The level of costumes this year was amazing; everywhere Kira looked she saw characters that could have stepped out of the movies. Of course there was the prerequisite whore costumes, young chippies in French maid and prostitute outfits, plus their male counterparts, but in general Kira was impressed.

She finally arrived at the bar and yelled her order over the thumping of the bass to the patch-wearing pirate bartender. While she waited she scanned the room; within seconds her heartbeat sped up as she laid eyes on Dom. He wore a pinstripe zoot suit and a black fedora; in his hands he carried a tommy gun. She knew she shouldn't be surprised by how good he looked in a suit but she was nonetheless. The wide shoulders tapered to a narrow waist, emphasizing his chest and arm muscles in a way that made Kira's insides stand up and sing.

He scanned the room, face slightly in shadow from the brim of his fedora. Kira felt it like a punch to the gut when his eyes touched on her. She was ever so grateful for the face mask she wore now, which hid her flushed cheeks and glazed eyes.

"Hey!" The voice finally penetrated through the fog that was Kira's brain. She turned and saw the bartender waving his hand impatiently at her drink.

"Sorry." She muttered and fumbled with her gloved hands to grab the twenty from her pocket. After she got her change she turned back to the bar, drink in hand, and suppressed a groan of dismay—Dom was gone.

She slipped the straw through the specially designed hole in her mask and rescanned the room, head bobbing to the music. She consoled herself with the knowledge that he was here and she would get her chance to talk to him.

The crowd surged in time to the loud music, pulsing as the floor vibrated beneath them. Kira felt the bass of the music inside her, throbbing with each beat, making her sway her hips slightly along with everyone else.

A voice close to her ear caught her off guard as it growled through her. "Bounty hunter. Are you here for someone in particular?"

She turned a smile that only she knew was there on her lips. The smart-assed quip she had been about to toss out died on her lips as she stared into a pair of incredible blue eyes.

She managed to recover enough to speak. "It's good to see that someone knows their Star Wars villains."

"I wouldn't call this character a villain. After all, it was Princess Leia in disguise trying to save Hans Solo. Are you a princess under the disguise?" Up close, Kira noticed the details in his costume, including the fake scar that graced his normally flawless cheek.

"I don't know if I'd say princess per se. I think I am more a true bounty hunter." Kira's voice was tinny sounding through the mask. "So I am looking for one of the Hutts. The reward for their capture is rather significant, and I would be willing to share with a certain mobster in a fabulous zoot suit."

Dom grinned, his eyes sparkling in the dim lighting. "Well I just wanted to pass on my congratulations on a costume well done." He turned to go.

"Dom." His name tore from her throat. "Don't go. I came to talk to you."

A frown flitted across his face. "I'm afraid you have me at a disadvantage, ma'am. You know who I am, and yet with your mask I am not sure who you are."

Kira nodded. "I understand. But can we go somewhere"—she paused—"quieter to talk?"

Dom nodded and led the way through the crowd, heading towards the staff area. The people parted for him, his air of authority and height making everyone immediately move out of his way. They quickly crossed the room and slipped through the swinging door, into the kitchen. The music was still very pervasive here, so Dom continued down a hallway off to the left. From his pocket he pulled out a key and unlocked one of the doors.

Inside was a small, crowded office sporting two chairs, a desk that was covered in precariously balanced stacks of paper, and two overflowing shelving units. He motioned towards one chair and sat himself on the edge of his desk, avoiding toppling one of the piles of paperwork easily. It was crowded, hot, and cramped. Kira barely noticed her surroundings or the heat, as she couldn't tear her gaze from Dom.

"So. You wanted to talk to me in private. Here we are. Are you going to tell me who you are?"

Kira swallowed a nervous mouthful of saliva and took a deep breath while reaching up and undoing her mask. She easily pulled it off and flicked her sweat-dampened hair back off her forehead. Slowly she raised her gaze to meet his, wary of what she might see in his eyes. His bright gaze flickered from her face to her hair and back to meet her eyes once more.

"Hi," she whispered.

"Kira." His lips curved into a slight smile, his eyes brightened.

"I didn't want to catch you off guard, but I was afraid you wouldn't see me if I called first." Her voice was quiet.

"No matter what happened between us, or didn't for that matter, I would never turn you away. I would have hoped you would know that. First, I want to take a second to apologize for my harsh words last time I saw you. You were in an incredibly hard place and I didn't help the situation, so I apologize." He easily expressed his feelings before holding up his forefinger, preventing her from speaking. "Before you get mad at me, I really like your hair."

Kira ran her fingers through the still styled locks that were now back to a natural shade of brown, laced with caramels and blondes. It was a colour Kira loved, making her feel beautiful. It suited her in a way the red never had. "Thank you," she whispered with a soft smile.

"So what did you come to say to me?" Dom pressed his hands together.

"I...." Kira took another deep breath, centering herself. "I'm sorry. I guess I wasn't as prepared to see you as I thought I was."

"You look great too." Dom leaned slightly towards her, opening the floor for her to talk. "What have you been doing the last month?"

Kira smiled in gratitude; he was making it so easy for her to talk. She said, "When I left here, I had originally planned to go to Michael and to try to make our relationship work." Dom flinched slightly before he recovered and maintained a serene façade, so Kira continued. "That's not what ended up happening. I went to see him, and realized I couldn't choose either of you. That I had to choose myself. So that's what I did. I choose me. I walked away from Michael, after being honest about sleeping with you. I faced my faults and I didn't hide from my flaws. I've spent the last thirty days getting to know me and what I want, what I like and who I want to be. I probably should take even longer, but I feel ready."

She paused, her eyes scanning Dom's face with interest, trying to judge if he understood what she said. Satisfied with what she saw, she spoke again.

"It's not that I didn't want you. It's that I needed to be the person I never was. I went from a child to a wife to a divorcée with no stops to discover me. I like the person I've become. I'm settled and able to think about an equal relationship with someone. I was hoping you were still interested in dating me, but if you aren't or you are already in a relationship, that's okay. I understand." She began to babble. "I didn't want to leave things the way they had been left. I wanted to talk to you, to smooth things over. To apologize for everything."

As she babbled, Dom stood suddenly, stilling her rapidly running mouth. He grabbed her upper arms, pulled her to her feet, and planted his soft lips against hers. With a sigh Kira melted into his body, her thoughts stilled, and the pure passion that had always flared between them ruled her. Automatically her hands looped around his neck and pulled him close. Lust led them down a path that had them panting and twisting against each other.

Finally they pulled apart and Dom whispered, "I've been waiting for you. I wanted to come to you, but I knew you needed the time to come to a decision on your own. I also had to do some soul searching. Last year, I was afraid to love again, and then I met you. In your arms I glimpsed the future, the dream. Without you, I am nothing. I exist, but I do not live. I don't want anyone else, and without you there is no one left. I'm all yours. *Mio amore*, my darling, *voglio stare sempre con ta.*"

Kira looked at him questioningly until he translated. "I always want to be with you."

"And I want to be with you too," she whispered back.

The End

THANK YOU FOR READING!

Dear Reader,

I hope you enjoyed *Becoming Kira*. I loved creating the characters of both Kira and Dom, even Michael was fun to create. I wanted to write a novella about a woman who wasn't perfect, who was a little 'long in the tooth' when it comes to romance novels, because romance doesn't stop just because we have passed the ripe age of thirty. Kira felt like someone I knew, like a relatable everyday woman who has been given a second chance at love.

As an author I love feedback, frankly I live for feedback. It helps me when writing to know the things that you loved and even the things you hated. I write for myself (because I have to write). But, I also write for you and I want it to be the best experience possible.

Finally, I need to ask a favor. If you are so inclined, I'd love a review of *Becoming Kira*. An honest review, I can't improve if I don't know what you liked and didn't like. I'd just truly enjoy your feedback.

As you may have heard, reviews are tough to come by these days. You, the reader, have the power to make or break a book. If you have the time, please head on over to amazon, and give a short (or long) review just plop Gloria C Bishop in the search bar and you'll find me.

Again, thank you so much for reading *Becoming Kira* and for spending time in my world.

In gratitude,

gloria C Bishop

gloriacbishop@gmail.com

Other titles by Gloria C. Bishop

If you liked *Becoming Kira* check out Gloria C. Bishop's other title available now:

Anna is your average small town girl. She likes to cook works at a bookstore, and is quiet, and klutzy -the girl next door. She is also a supernatural creature. Becoming a zombie has brought her nothing but heartache. Her family life, her love life, even her self-esteem have been shattered as a result of her transformation. After sitting on the sidelines for far too long, Anna decides to begin dating again. Unfortunately her foray into the world of supernatural singledom is met with disaster. Thrown into the arms of the one man who hurt her more than any other by a psychopath bent on her destruction, Anna is forced to reevaluate her opinion of Nathan. Their steamy chemistry is overwhelming as they discover that together the can find, and overcome, the fiend who is behind the attempts on Anna's life.

ABOUT THE AUTHOR

This is that whole "bio" section that always gets me, I never know what to say. I'm Gloria, the one in that picture. Hello! *gives a little grin and a wave.* Anyways enough chatting lets give this whole "about me" section a go. I was born and raised in small town southwestern Ontario in a family of extra-large proportions. I have two sisters and two brothers and so many aunts and uncles my hubby still can't keep track of them. I am an avid reader, gobbling up four books a week. I read everything from romance, to fantasy to paranormal. I started writing early and have never stopped. Also a self professed geek my fandoms include The Princess Bride, Firefly (well anything Joss Whedon), zombies and more. I am happily married to the man of my dreams and we live with our two teenagers kids and a slightly overweight cockapoo named Spike. I love connecting with fans, find me on Facebook at www.facebook.com/gloriabishopauthor or my blog at www.gloriacbishop.blogspot.ca

www.ingramcontent.com/pod-product-compliance
Lightning Source LLC
Chambersburg PA
CBHW070223140626

46555CB00018B/1257

* 9 7 8 0 9 9 4 0 8 0 5 0 9 *